Patric LeClerc is surrounded by darkness from both without and within. Blinded many years before in a tragic accident, he does nothing but drive everyone away with his anger and resentment over his misfortunes.

Everyone, that is, except Callie Carpenter. Desperate for a home and a job after the break-up of her dreadful marriage to the wealthy but abusive Jason, she tries to restore Dark Gardens Plantation to its former glory.

But soon it isn't only the housework she becomes interested in, as Patric lets his guard down and shows her that deep within, a spark of warmth and humanity still glows. When Jason threatens to take away the only thing precious to her, her son Cameron, Callie and Patric join forces to try to save the boy.

But can Patric's dark past ever allow him to see Callie's love for him, or will he drive her away as well, for having come too close to the true, if vulnerable, Patric LeClerc?

"A superb novel, sensually atmospheric. Patric is a grim and forbidding hero at first, but he soon evokes our sympathy with the harsh way he has been treated, and in turn treats others because he does not know any better. The author deals seriously with issues of handicap and abuse, but also with forgiveness, recovery, and above all, the healing power of love.

"Callie too is well-drawn, learning to stand on her own two feet for the first time, but paralyzed with fear by her controlling ex-husband. But her love for her son, and her growing love for Patric make her whole again. Though there are other complications in their lives which seem almost insurmountable, the climax pulls all of the tensions within the novel together into a completely satisfying whole."
Michael Brennan, author of *Campaign for Love*

"Wonderful! Patric definitely has shades of Mr. Rochester from *Jane Eyre* in him. Disappointed by the world and convinced that no one could ever really love him for himself, he is locked away in a prison of his own making until Callie and her young son Cameron re-humanize him. The clever twists and turns in the plot keep you on tenterhooks to see if love will indeed find a way with this tormented pair, but the ending will leave you delighted."
Evelyn Trimborn, author of *Heedless Hearts*

Karen L. Williams

If you are ever in Arlington, TX you might consider looking up romance author Karen Williams. With her writing career on the move, she still makes time to talk shop in her bookstore—> shameless promotion ...www.txbookshelf.com (The BookShelf) and help other fledgling writers break into the business via Rhapsody Magazine, an online e-zine she co-edits with fellow author, Cathy McDavid. Ms. Williams uses her bookstore and Rhapsody Magazine as a way of promoting and supporting the genres as well as fulfilling another of her lifelong goals.

You can visit Ms. Williams at the website www.spotlighters.com/williams.html or E-mail her at txbookshelf@netzero.net

Also by the author

The Wings of Love
Crazy For You, Volume Two of the *Cajun Hearts* series

As Alexis Hart
Moonlight for Maggie, Volume One of the *Cajun Hearts* series

This book is dedicated to Moghis in thanks for faith, trust, friendship, love.

Also, heartfelt thanks to Carolyn Rogers, who has done everything in her power to be my very dear friend and a true source of inspiration. Thank you for every nudge, push, and pep talk when the world had closed in on me. I only hope I can do half as much for you as you have done for me.

DARK SHINES MY LOVE

Karen L. Williams

Domhan Books

Copyright USA, UK and Worldwide the author 2000

All rights reserved. No part of this book may be reproduced or transmitted in any form by any means, electronic or mechanical, including photocopying, recording, or by any information and storage retrieval system, without permission in writing from the copyright owner.

This is a work of fiction. Names, characters, places and incidents are the product of the author's imagination, and any resemblance to any actual persons, living or dead, events, or locales, is entirely coincidental.

ISBN: 1-58345-585-X Rocket
1-58345-586-8 paper
1-58345-673-2 Microsoft
1-58345-675-9 hardcover
1-58345-680-5 large format hardcover
1-58345-681-3 large format paperback
1-58345-674-0 Glassbook
1-58345-676-7 ION

Published by Domhan Books
9511 Shore Road, Suite 514
Brooklyn New York 11209

Printer by Lightning Source, TN
Distributed by Ingram Book Company

PROLOGUE

December 24, 1975
Garden View Plantation, Louisiana

Heart-rending shrieks filled the Louisiana night. *"Why are you doing this to me?"*

Patric covered his ears, struggling to block out his parents' angry shouts.

"I swear to you, Lucia. Nothing happened. This is all a huge mistake."

"How can you deny what I saw with my own eyes?"

"I am *not* having an affair with her. She came out here after me. Just as I told her to go back into the party, she kissed me. I have no feelings for her."

"Get out!"

His father took a long pull from his cocktail glass then flung it. The glass sailed through the air. Patric ducked down behind the old sofa just in time. There was a crash over his head. Shards of glass rained over him and slid down inside the collar of his red-checked flannel shirt. He covered his face with his hands and fought back the tears. No matter how much he wanted to cry out, he couldn't let his father catch him spying.

"Why do you always have to resort to violence when you don't get your own way?"

He listened to his mother's sobs and longed to run

out and comfort her, but he knew that would earn him a beating.

"Why won't you listen to me when I'm telling you the truth?"

"Don't you dare try to make this out to be my fault. I'm not the one who's doing God knows what with the entire town."

"That's it. I'm through trying to explain things."

He strode across the balcony through the garden. His boot-heels clicked on the brick pathway, and the smell of his father's cologne lingered after he passed. Fearing he might come back, he resisted the urge to look over the back of the sofa, and held himself perfectly still.

"Where are you going? I'm not finished yet!"

Patric's father turned. "Lucia, your melodrama bores me. I told you nothing was going on, and I meant it."

"Liar! How many times have you told me the same thing?"

"Lucia. Enough! Go back in to the party and we'll discuss this later. You have a son who needs his mother at Christmas."

To Patric, the silence said more than the hurtful words. He waited for his mother to say something, but she remained silent.

A chill crept the length of his spine and he shivered. He closed his eyes and curled up tighter against himself. Silently, tears fell from his eyes as slivers of the shattered glass scraped against his flesh. The cool night air blew across the balcony and cooled the moist drops of his father's whiskey on Patric's back. He waited.

"This is it, Michael. After tonight you'll never do this to me again. I'm taking Patric and we're leaving."

Patric's sadness turned to joy. "Oh, Mother!" He

gave up his hiding place behind the old battered sofa and ran to his mother.

All heads turned to him. His gaze turned to the woman standing in the shadows.

"Go inside, Paddy." His mother's voice quivering, her pain obvious, drew him toward her like a magnet.

He ran to her side and hugged her waist. "Can we really leave, Mother?"

"No. Go inside."

His father's voice echoed as the palm of his father's hand slammed into Patric's head. He fell on the ground, hard. The corner of a square terra-cotta planter dug into his forehead and blood trickled down into his eye. Patric held in the fear as his father advanced on him.

Anger flashed in his father's eyes. "Get up!"

"I'm sorry, Father, I didn't mean to hear. I was trying to see the other guests through the window, and you came out."

"It's all right, Paddy. No one is angry with you. Just run inside and Mama will be in soon." She leaned forward and extended her hand to help him up.

"No, you won't make him a sissy! You coddle him like a fragile little girl. He's a boy, and if you take him away he'll never become a man."

"I'll take him away and he'll be whatever he wants."

"You are so wrong, Lucia. Neither of you will ever leave Garden View. You'll never leave *me*."

Unable to stand the cruelty of his father's words, Patric climbed to his feet and ran. He ran as fast as his legs would carry him, and as far as they could go. It wasn't until he reached the bank of the river that he collapsed onto the damp grass. The cool moisture soaked through his shirt and jeans and he shivered.

He rolled onto his back and hundreds of tiny nerve points prickled. He stared up at the vast darkness of the sky. Where were the stars? Why couldn't he find the moon? Those and so many more questions crowded his mind. Closing his eyes, he fought against the pain wearing him down. Patric lay on the bank of the Mississippi River and willed the night to be over.

How could his parents have been so cruel, and at Christmas too? Why had his father said such horrible things to his mother? His beautiful, kind and loving mother, the belle of New Orleans?

Pain throbbed in his back. His shoulders stung for reasons he didn't understand. His body ached, from pain and loneliness. Fear. Never in his ten short years of life could he remember being so afraid. The fear made him angry. He could hear his father's voice in his mind. "Fear is unacceptable."

Clenching his fists, Patric lay in the wet grass and prayed for the last time. *Please God, make it all stop.*

CHAPTER ONE

December 1999
Dark Gardens Plantation, Louisiana

"Get the hell out of my house!"
"But Mr. LeClerc, I didn't know it wasn't allowed."
"How could you think I would pay you to do God knows what with your boyfriend in my house?"

Patric LeClerc fought against the level of pain rising in his head. He collapsed into the dining room chair and lowered his head to rest against his forearms.

"Are you all right, Sir?"
"Get me my damned pills and then get out."

He rubbed his hand across his mouth and sighed. "Tell the service to send the next incompetent over."

He listened to the retreating footsteps grow softer as the nurse hurried down the long corridor. She weighed considerably more than the last nurse they'd sent, and the rapid clicking of her heels indicated her to be shorter as well. The scent of lilacs lingered in the air. The cloying fragrance only intensified the pounding in his temples. He clutched his head and struggled to gain control of his pain. *Calm.* He had to calm down or the throbbing would only increase. If he intended to do anything other than sleep his life away, he needed to get a grip on things. He leaned back in his chair, more than a little tired of feeling sorry for himself, but unsure how to change the inevitable.

What the hell did it matter? He'd lived alone for so long, he wouldn't know what to do with a real life anyway, even if he had a second chance. His self-pity flooded through him, yet he cursed himself for being a pathetic fool. The only people who even knew he was alive knew or even cared, were from the blasted medical agency his attorney had insisted he hire nurses from.

Clicking echoed in his head, only it wasn't just in his head. He sensed the nurse as she entered the room. He gritted his teeth and waited for her to hand him his pills. The shadow of a hand passed in front of him, then moved back and forth before disappearing.

"Just put the damn things down and leave me alone." He waited for the tap of the prescription bottle hitting against the table. Silence. "Are you deaf?"

"Sir, I was told not to leave you alone. I'll lose my job if I go."

Patric gritted his teeth against the annoying hum in her voice buzzing in his ears. "That's where you're wrong. I pay your salary, and you've already lost your job."

The pill bottle slammed against the table, ringing out like a gunshot. Struggling against the pain beating behind his eyes, he felt for the bottle. His hands trembled and knocked against the bottle. Several of the tiny pills scattered onto the table.

"Blast it." He brushed his hand across the wooded table, searching for his relief. Finally, his fingertip brushed against a tablet. Desperate, he picked it up with an unsteady hand and shoved the pill into his mouth.

Patric grimaced at bitter aftertaste, then laid his head back down and waited for his reprieve, small as it would be. His mood dipped dangerously low as his mind replayed the aroused groans of his former nurse. What the hell right did she have to be enjoying herself on his time? What right did anyone have to be happy? God, he couldn't even remember what a woman's body felt like. He drifted to sleep, exhausted by the intensity of his own self-pity, anger and loathing.

Several hours later, Patric woke up. Alone. Before he could get his bearings, the shrill ringing of the telephone startled him. He ignored it. If Alexander Graham Bell were alive, he'd gladly strangle him. In the mood he was in, the last thing he needed was to talk to any one.

The windshield wipers on Callie's old-model Volvo scraped futilely across the window. *I must be insane.* The wind and rain whipped around, and she struggled to keep control of the car. Then the road curved. She gaped at the monstrosity standing ominously dark in the middle of a grove. Dark Gardens Plantation. *Home.* The single word struck her as peculiar. She'd never called any place home, and yet, the word came to her mind as she stared at the vast house.

Lightning flashed up toward the sky, granting her a better look at the hell house, as her boss had referred to it. Black shutters covered floor to ceiling windows along the front of the house. The double doors stood dead center in the middle of the house at the top of a ridiculously long flight of stairs. Why would anyone build a house you had to walk up so many steps to get into?

Callie pushed her remaining questions aside and shifted the car into gear. The answers didn't matter. She wasn't here to like it. She was here because she didn't have anywhere else to go. As she got closer to the house, **her feelings of trepidation only increased.**

"Geez, I think I took a wrong turn and ended up in Transylvania."

A small gray kitten purred a vague response and poked its nose out of the hole Callie had cut for him in the top of the box. When her life had fallen apart, she'd been able to save only two things. She looked down at Mardi and smiled. The small kitten had managed to get locked out of her apartment while everything had been going on and had been saved from a fate worse than— well he had been saved. Now at least she had her clothes, and two priceless treasures. And a roof over her head.

She glanced up at the house. Shaking her head, she concentrated on navigating the gravel driveway. She peered out the window and looked at the surrounding landscape. "Kinda dark out here, Mardi. You gonna be okay?"

Meow.

"I am not afraid of the dark. How could you say that?"

Meow.

"I know it's just a gloomy house, but have you seen how big it is?" Callie laughed. "Of course you haven't. You're in a box."

Purr.

"Soon, baby. We're almost there and then I'll let you out. No more boxes for you. With a house this size, it's party time for Mardi Gras." She rubbed the small pink nose poking from inside the box.

By the time she parked the car in front of the house, the rain had lessened to little more than an annoying drizzle. Not enough to matter, only enough to get her wet. But her black and white polka-dotted slicker would be enough to keep her dry.

She stepped out of the car and leaned against the roof, awe-struck. In spite of the six white pillars adorning the front of the house, it looked more like an over-sized mausoleum than a plantation. All she knew about Dark Gardens was that its owner was blind and obsessively reclusive. Her report said he hadn't been out of his house in over eight years. Thankfully, he'd remained mostly self-sufficient. Her job would entail cleaning, cooking and companionship. She would make good money and they'd have a roof over their heads.

"Well, Mardi. Let's go."

Meow.

"Yeah, I hope he's awake too."

Callie rang the bell again. She'd been standing on the porch for going on ten minutes and hadn't even heard a rustle from inside. Finally, she twisted the knob, thankful when it turned.

"Hello. Mr. LeClerc? Are you home?" *Of course he's home you ninny. He's a recluse.* "My name is Callie Carpenter. I'm your new nurse."

She stepped into the entry-way and waited for her eyes to adjust to the darkness. The front foyer held no decoration or furniture. She saw a doorway directly to the left and another directly to the right. Both doors hung slightly ajar. No light came from either. Several more steps in and she saw it.

Lightning sparked, and the grandest staircase she'd ever seen flashed before her. The wide steps ascended to a platform that branched off in either direction. Then it struck her. The lightning had flashed above the staircase. **She set her box down on the floor next to her. "I'll be right back, Mardi."**

When her foot landed on the first step, an odd sense of foreboding seized her. Attributing it to nerves, she continued up. When she reached the landing, she looked up. Centered above the stairs, hung an enormous crystal chandelier. Suspended from beams under a magnificent skylight, it dangled in ominous brilliance. "Incredible."

Her breath caught in her throat and she couldn't tear her eyes away.

She jumped when she heard a thump behind her. "Mr. LeClerc is that you? I'm the new nurse."

"Stop yelling. I'm blind, not deaf."

The cold brusque tone sent a shiver creeping up the length of her spine. She could barely discern his shadow at the foot of the stairs. She moved toward him, but he walked away. When she reached the last step, she caught a glimpse of his back before he disappeared into a room. Quickly, she checked on Mardi before following her new employer into the room.

Like the main room, this room held no light. A few steps into the room she bumped into a small table. "Do you mind if I turn on a light?"

"Yes, I do," he snapped. "What do you want?"

"I'm the new nurse. The agency told me I needed to be out here tonight. I tried to call before I came, but no one answered, so I packed my things and drove out."

"Well, bully for you, Mrs. Cartwright."

Sarcasm swam around her as he spoke. "My name is Callie Carpenter, and its Miss."

"Whatever your name is, I don't need a damned nurse. So you can take yourself and your things and go home." She heard him move in the far corner of the room, but still couldn't see him clearly.

"I wish I could," she whispered softly.

"Then do it!"

She gasped at his harshness; surprised he'd heard her. "I'm sorry I said that. It's just—I don't have any place to go."

"That's not my problem. Now get out."

Callie could almost hear his teeth grinding against one another. Her eyes blinked with each clipped word he spoke. She wondered if he weren't in pain. Her sympathetic nature justified his rude behavior, and she chalked it up to loneliness.

"Sir, I need this job. I don't have any family to go to and I don't have an apartment anymore. I'd appreciate it if you'd at least give me a chance to prove I can do this job."

She stood in the darkness listening to the silence for several minutes. Finally, she heard him move.

"Whether you can do the job or not is of no consequence. I'm sure you are quite capable. The point is I don't want you here."

"Then why does the agency keep sending people out here?"

"Miss Carson, I've lived in this house for most of my life, and I assure you I can take care of myself." He paused. "You are here because of some twisted sense of loyalty on my attorney's part."

"I have no doubt about that, Mr. LeClerc. I'm not actually here to take care of you. I guess I am more of a housekeeper than a nurse. A maid if you will. The fact of the matter is, I need this job. And the name is Carpenter."

Callie knew she didn't need to beg. If he made her leave she could get another assignment. It might not offer her a place to live, but she'd manage some how.

But she found herself wanting to stay and find out more about this mysterious man. Her ex-husband, Jason, would accuse her of living in another of her Florence Nightingale fantasies, but there was just something about Patric LeClerc….

Maybe because she hadn't actually seen her new boss yet, or maybe because of the house he lived in, whichever, she would convince him to let her stay. "I really would like to stay."

"I'd really like you to go," he returned.

"But Mr. LeClerc—"

"You seem to be under the mistaken impression that I am the Salvation Army and that I care about you being homeless." He hesitated before he went on, and Callie cut in.

"No, Sir, you are not a charity organization." *You'd need a heart to be that.* "I only hope-

"Lets get something straight right now, Miss Carter. This is my house and you will stay the hell out of my way."

"Yes, Sir."

"If you so much as breath in my space, you're out of here," he snarled.

Callie sighed a breath of relief. He had given in. She could stay. "It will only take me a minute to bring in my belonging."

"Your room will be at the top of the left wing. Second door. If you need anything, get it yourself."

"I'll have to go back into town in the morning to pick up a few more things and take care of some business. Is it okay if I bring my—"

"Bring whatever you have to. Just remember that you have the left side of the stairs and I have the right.

Stay out of my way."

"And it's Carpenter, Mr. LeClerc. Callie Carpenter."

Callie stepped forward to thank him. But at the same time a door closed across the room and then she shut her mouth. He'd walked out and left her standing alone. She hadn't even seen his face.

She switched on a lamp and looked around the room. She noticed the sparse furnishings and justified the reason. Maybe since he's sight impaired he doesn't like a lot of things in the way. *He just doesn't like anything.*

"I know," he whispered softly.

Patric stood inside the tunnel listening to her move around the room. He saw the shadow of the table light she'd turned on. He leaned against the panel and let the cool wood ease his tension.

She was different. He couldn't quite figure out how, but he sensed she wouldn't be as easily bullied as the others before her. He'd definitely heard fear in her voice, but he sensed it as a confident fear. A week or two would do little to interfere with his hectic schedule. *Yeah right.*

His body acknowledged her presence on the other side of the slide panel, and he remained perfectly still. He took several steadying breaths struggling to tamp down the waves of desire coursing through him. The secret door vibrated as her hand rested on the cool wood. He could almost feel her touch on his shoulder.

None of the other idiots from the agency had yet discovered the locations of his secret panels, but he had a feeling he'd need to be more careful with Miss Callie Carpenter. He'd tried to get more of a sense of her, but she hadn't gotten close enough.

When he heard the study door click shut, he made his way down the narrow corridor and up the stairs to his room. Not bothering to turn on the light, he stripped off his jeans and T-shirt and crawled into bed. As he lay on top of the crisp sheets, he listened to the house.

Even from across the building he could hear her moving around in her quarters. The floorboard at the foot of her bed creaked and she stopped. He knew she'd stopped because the next six boards also creaked. He'd meant to get them repaired, for nearly six years, but hadn't bothered. He'd seen no point in it.

Her bedroom door opened and she padded down the hallway. Where was she going? Probably off to snoop around the other rooms in the west wing. They all did it. One nurse had even stolen from him, but a few years in prison would cure her of that mistake.

Felling more relaxed than he had for a long time, Patric dozed off while listening for his new companion to return to her room.

Callie stepped into the kitchen and could barely believe her eyes. *What the hell have the other nurses been doing?*

Stacks of dirty dishes lay scattered around the massive cooking area. The room looked scarcely habitable.

She moved to the sink and reached down to turn on the water. "Oh-my-God." She covered her mouth and stepped back. She prayed she had the stomach to endure the mess. She silently cursed the former employees for their lack of ethics. How could they take this man's money when they had obviously been doing nothing? Well perhaps a letter to the employee advisor would be in order....

Mardi brushed up against her ankle. "No, baby, you can't come up here." He purred and wrapped his soft tail around her leg.

"Oh no you don't, pal." She bent and picked up the kitten, cuddling it to her cheek. "This place isn't fit for either of us, but since I'm getting paid, I'll stay and clean it up."

She set the cat down outside the swinging door and shooed him away. He could go off and investigate on his own while she scoured the scum off weeks worth of dishes. As she cleaned, she periodically stopped to add another item to her shopping list.

She found mountains of garbage, certainly not from anything wholesome, and no food in the pantry. She wondered how her patient had survived.

When she finally put the last dish away, her watch read five o'clock. She'd worked straight through the night and had to be back in town before nine. She switched off the kitchen light and went in search of Mardi. She found him asleep on a velvet chair in the study. It was the only room he had been able get into, since all the other doors were tightly shut.

"Come on, sweetheart. Let's get some sleep before we go take care of business." She picked up the purring cat and walked to her room.

The sound of her employer's scolding voice pulled her from a sound sleep. "Miss Carpenter, would breakfast be too much to ask?"

She opened her eyes and looked for him. She lay in her bed, alone in her room, but still she heard his voice. She looked over at the intercom box on her bedside table and pressed the button.

"I'll be right there. I'm sorry."

"Just put a box of cereal and the milk in the dining

room. I'll be down there when I'm ready."

"Yes, Sir." *On the double, sir.*

"Don't get up, honey. I'll feed the baby."

Mardi stretched across the extra pillow and Callie crawled out of bed. "At least since Mr. LeClerc is blind, it won't matter if I don't wear a uniform."

She pulled a pair of leggings and a sweater out of her suitcase and quickly pulled a comb through her hair. She stopped in front of the vanity mirror. *Good thing he's blind. No one should have to look at hair this drab shade of brown.* "Maybe once we get on our feet, Mardi, I'll get a new hairdo and a flea collar for you."

Meow.

"Yeah, I know, I'm the last of the big spenders." She leaned down and scratched Mardi's ear. "Go back to sleep, lazy bones."

Callie didn't find Patric in the dining room, so she left his breakfast on the table. She did find a credit card on the table. The intercom speaker on the wall crackled to life and she waited for his next command.

"Take that card and buy what you need to get by for a few weeks. I assume there are no cleaning supplies or food."

She waited.

"I'll take care of my own dishes when I'm finished with breakfast."

Silence.

She pressed the button and spoke softly. "I'm going into town now to get the supplies and the rest of my things. Do you need anything special?"

"Peace and privacy."

"Yes, Sir."

At half past eight, Callie pulled away from the house.

She drove away from the plantation and watched it grow smaller in her rear view mirror. She noticed the curtain in one of the upstairs windows flutter. She slowed her car, hoping to catch a glimpse of the mysterious man she worked for, and lived with, but he didn't step forward. Was he watching her? *Of course not, he's blind.*

Patric listened as the car drove farther away. Her small car needed a new muffler. He noticed the rain had stopped, and he leaned against the window, letting the cool glass chill him. He couldn't stop himself from wondering what business she had in town, or why she needed this job so desperately. She had to be desperate. She'd spent Lord knows how long cleaning the kitchen until it smelled fresh as spring. He'd gone in there several times to do it himself, but each time had found he didn't have the stomach for it.

Carefully, he made his way downstairs. When he sat in his chair he found a bowl and spoon sitting on a cloth place mat in front of him. He'd forgotten he had the place mats. Further investigation uncovered a cloth napkin, a bowl of peaches and some kind of grain cereal. For the first time in months he poured cold milk into his bowl and enjoyed breakfast.

When he stood up to take care of his dishes, something unfamiliar slipped around his leg. "A cat! She's brought a damn cat into my house."

He plunked back down in his chair and took several deep breaths. He winced against the throbbing in his temple. *What right did she have?*

Meow.

"So, now I have to tolerate her, and you?"

He sighed as the small kitten leaped into his lap. The tiny body vibrated against his stomach as it purred.

"Don't bother being friendly. Neither of you will be staying."

Purr.

Patric lifted the kitten up and held him against his chest. "I'm not going to change my mind, so forget about it." When the small animal snuggled up to his cheek, he relaxed. The throbbing in his head subsided.

He didn't have any idea how long the kitten lay against him before it finally fell asleep in his hands. He sat at the dining room table until he heard the muffler of Callie's car. He set the kitten down gently on a chair and hurriedly moved to put his dishes in the kitchen. He closed the secret panel just as she stepped through the kitchen door.

"Well, what are you up to Mardi? You haven't been in Mr. LeClerc's way, have you?"

The kitten's purring and meowing grew louder, and Patric new she was petting the cat. Mardi? At least now he knew what to call the animal. Well, maybe it wouldn't be so bad having the little fellow around. He'd never had a pet before, and the idea gave him an odd sense of loss and longing. He heard his father's voice in the back of his mind. *"Animals are bothersome and disgusting creatures. I feed you and your mother, isn't that enough?"*

"Want some milk, Mardi? Here you go, sweetie."

The soft tinkling sound of Callie's voice reminded him of the wind instruments in the symphonies he listened to. Maybe a clarinet. Soft, yet bold enough to demand attention. It carried through the room, yet remained delicate. He shifted his weight from one leg to another. A board creaked under his foot.

"Mr. LeClerc, is that you?"

He held himself perfectly still. Why didn't he know

that board creaked? He knew every sound in the house. At least he thought he did. She'd distracted him. That had to be it. But why? *She's just a nurse. Someone who gets paid to live in my house and invade my privacy. Someone who smelled like rose water.*

He listened to her move around the kitchen putting things away. He heard her pull a chair across the room to prop the pantry door open. He'd meant to fix it that too.

"So, Mardi, have you met our boss?"

Patric listened as the kitten continued to lap up the milk in his saucer.

"So, are you going to tell me what he looks like? Is he big and hairy with warts all over his face?"

Meow.

"Holding back are you? Well, after living inside this house for so many years he's probably like a ghost. What do you think made him become a recluse, Mardi?"

So, she thought he was an old ogre. What would she think if she knew he'd barely hit thirty-four? Hardly old. Well, he didn't have any warts, but he surely didn't stand a chance in any beauty contest. He rubbed his hand across his chin and realized it had been too long since he'd attempted to shave. He probably did look like an ogre. Then again, what did it matter? He wasn't out to impress anyone. If she didn't like the way he looked she could take herself and her cat and find another job. Silently, he told himself he would shave because he needed it and not because of her. He turned and began to walk upstairs.

Suddenly he heard an even more high-pitched voice. "Mommy, can I go look upstairs?"

Patric froze in his tracks.

CHAPTER TWO

"Cameron, hush. I asked you to be quiet until I tell Mr. LeClerc about you."

"Mom, I stayed in that room for a while, but I don't want to read any more."

Callie pulled her son up against her. He was the most important thing in her life and she hated to see him unhappy.

"I looked for a television, but there ain't one."

"There isn't one," she gently corrected.

"That's what I said."

"No, you said ain't."

"I know, there ain't no TV."

"Oh, never mind. After I get my first pay check we'll see about buying a small one."

"What am I supposed to do until then?"

Callie reached into a bag and pulled out a box. "Take this and go investigate outside."

"Cool, Mom. It's a Walkman, with a cassette player."

"I know, I bought it for you." She watched her son tear open the box. "It's not brand new. I bought it at a pawn shop. It's all we can afford. But the owner threw in a couple of cassettes."

"Way cool, Mom."

"They're out in the glove box of the car. You can look around the grounds, but don't go into any of the buildings, and don't cross any fences."

"Oh, all right." He grabbed an apple out of the bag and ran out the door.

"I love you, Cameron."

"I know, Mom. Me too." Then he disappeared.

Patric didn't bother to be quiet. It didn't matter if she found the secret tunnel. He wanted her out, along with her menagerie. No sweet smelling liar would come in and take over his house. He brushed his hand along the wall until he found the latch. He pushed the door open and stepped into the study.

The warmth of sunlight filtered in and settled on his arm. For a moment he enjoyed the feel of heat as it warmed the shirt resting against his arm. He imagined himself sitting out on the lawn. He remembered the colorful birds fluttering around the skies above him—then he realized.

She'd opened the curtains. What the hell was she doing? These drapes hadn't been pulled in at least five years. Twenty-six nurses and no one had even dared, or cared, for that matter. She'd been in his house for one night and she'd already started changing things. That wouldn't do. *No, that just won't do.*

"Carpenter, get in here." Patric stopped and stood in the middle of the room. Too much nervous energy made him pace the small area. What right did she have to come into his home and make him—*feel things*? He stopped in front of window and tried to remember how long it had been since the warmth of the sun had touched him. Had he missed it?

The squishing of her rubber-soled shoes brought him out of his silent musings. The sound stopped. The door to the library opened, then closed. Then the door to the study opened. He let himself lean against the wall in the corner. The element of surprise gave him an advantage.

"Mr. LeClerc, are you in here?"

"Where else would I be? Last I remember this is still my house, isn't it?"

She stood far too close. How had she gotten so far into the room without him hearing? So much for the element of surprise.

"You're—you're—not...."

"I'm what, Carpenter?"

She jumped when he yelled at her, the shadow of her body more visible than anything he'd seen in years. He turned toward the window and stared blankly at the sun's shadows. He couldn't see the details, but he could see her form, thin and petite. The darker shadow around her head told him she had long dark hair, worn down.

"You're—you're—"

"Spit it out, I don't have all day." *You have somewhere else to go?*

"Old," she mumbled.

"What?"

"No, not old. You're young."

"No I'm not old, and I'm not happy either. What the hell do you think you're doing?"

"I don't know what you mean."

Patric reached for the table and stepped closer to her. "I said stay out of my way."

"And I have."

"I said don't invade my space."

"And I haven't."

"No? Did you think I wouldn't notice a small furry beast roaming the house?"

She sniffed, and he turned away from her.

"Mardi is just a baby. I'll keep him closed in my room with me. I promise he won't be a problem."

Her voice soothed, even with the slight tremor in it. He'd frightened her; he heard it in her voice. A twinge of guilt shot through him. He remembered the other problem and his anger returned. "So, how did you expect to hide a child from me?"

She sat down and the cushion of the wing-back chair whooshed. He listened for the tell-tale signs of sobbing. He heard silence. Even the house stood quiet. No boards creaking, no shutters slamming. No settling noises from the foundation. No familiar sounds to soothe him. In one night, everything had changed. One small woman had screwed up what had taken him years to adjust to. A woman who smelled like rose water.

"Did you plan to keep him locked in your room with the cat? Don't you think that's a bit cruel?"

"Of course not. I would never—"

"Well, you won't have to."

"Mr. LeClerc, I tried to ask you last night if I could bring Cameron and you told me to bring whatever I needed."

"And you thought I meant a child?"

"He's the only thing I need. He's my son and I've already left him for one night too many. I'll not be separated from him again. I'm sorry if you have a problem with that."

"Your loyalty to your son is admirable, but it's none of my concern. You can be with your son wherever and whenever you choose."

"Thank you."

"Except here."

Callie wiped her nose on the sleeve of her sweater

and forced herself not to beg. She didn't know where she would go, but she wasn't going to stay in a house with a man with so much anger inside him. Cameron needed a better environment than this, anyway, a normal one for the first time in a long time.

"Fine. Give me a few minutes and I'll go."

She stiffly walked past him and left the room.

Alone in the kitchen, as she unpacked the grocery bags to see what she should take with her, she let her tears flow. This assignment had been her answer, her salvation. It would have solved all her problems. When Jason had thrown her out, he'd given her nothing but a few of her clothes and Cameron. This job would have offered her enough money to get a place of her own eventually. A place where Cameron could be happy and secure. A home. She remembered the odd feeling when she'd first seen the house. Now he'd ruined it all.

Callie began sorting through the dusty pantry, but her emotions got the better of her, and she sobbed aloud. Certain no one could hear her, she muttered out loud to herself, "Mean, nasty, vile-tempered pain in the—"

Wild eyes flashed in her memory. They had been stormy gray eyes filled with a tumultuous kind of sadness, which had contrasted magnificently with his pale gold skin, which she imagined must once have glowed with health until the accident that has left him with an indentation down the side of his face from temple to eye. But he certainly wasn't the Frankenstein she had pictured living in a haunted old mansion. No, on the contrary, he had been stunningly handsome, certainly the most striking man she had ever seen.

She imagined his strong, sculpted jaw under the growth of his beard. She remembered the wild ebony hair falling down around his shoulders, begging to be brushed and stroked, but no one stroked a porcupine with a healthy set of quills. She'd backed him into a corner and his razor sharp defenses had come up and cut her to the bone. She hoped for a moment, that all of the anger she'd seen in his eyes hadn't been directed at her.

"Mom, what's wrong?"

She jumped at the sound of Cameron's voice behind her. She hadn't heard him walk in. He stood in the doorway with his new headphones around his neck, a puzzled look of concern on his face.

"You're crying, Mom. Are you hurt?"

"No, honey, I'm not hurt. I need you to go back upstairs and start carrying your things down to the car."

"Why? I thought we lived here now. This place is really cool and I want to stay."

"Well, I guess you are under the mistaken impression that Mr. LeClerc cares what you, or I wants."

"He's kicking us out on your first day?" He turned and walked out of the kitchen. Before the door closed she heard him mumble, "He can't do that to my mom. I'll fix him."

"Cameron, no!"

"Where are you, you mean old troll?" Cameron ran up and down the halls yelling for the man who'd made his mom cry. "I know you're here. I want to see you."

Just inside the study, Cameron's feet skidded to a halt, bringing the lightweight carpet up with him. His bottom thudded onto the floor and he stared up at the giant man. Black hair stuck out everywhere, and the man had a longer beard than anyone he'd ever seen. For everything Cameron could remember, the person in front of him looked like every crazy man who'd ever killed kids in the movies he had watched at his best friend's house, against his mother's wishes.

"Are you looking for *me*?"

Cameron thought for a minute, and decided this couldn't be Mr. LeClerc. His mother took care of old people who couldn't take care of themselves. If this man couldn't take care of himself—

"No, I'm looking for the old man who made my mother cry."

"No one made your mother cry," Patric argued.

"I don't lie, sir."

The man let out a deep breath. "No one said you did."

"Yes, you did. You said no one made my mom cry."

"Look kid, what does this have to do with you lying?"

"Forget it." Cameron scooted back away from the man and stood up. "I want to talk to him about her job."

"What right do you have to interfere in your mother's business?"

Cameron pulled his shoulders back and stood as tall as he could. He stepped toward the man in a statement of courage. This man had to know he would protect his mother at all costs. "I'm the man of the family now, and that makes it my business."

"Is that so?" the man asked, rubbing the hair on his chin.

"Where's the boss?" Cameron hoped the man in front of him wouldn't try and block his path. He'd beat up Billy Marcus, but taking this man down would be too hard.

"I'm the boss."

Cameron stared. "You can't be. You're not old."

"So I've been told."

"I want the man my mom is supposed to take care of."

"I'm Patric LeClerc."

Cameron stared at him, then realized the man wasn't looking at him, in fact he wasn't looking at anything. Cameron waved his hand in front of the man's face.

"Stop that!"

The man reached out to grab his hand, but Cameron pulled away before he caught it. He stepped away and considered running.

"I'm not totally blind. I can still see enough to know you're making fun of me."

"Am not. I just didn't know you couldn't see."

"Now you do."

The hulk of a man straightened himself, and glared down at Cameron. Glazed eyes bore into him and Cameron stepped back.

"So, you're the man mom came to take care of. If you can't see, why are you making her leave?"

"I don't owe you any explanations. It's my house and I can do anything I damn well please."

"Mom says it's not polite to swear." Cameron took another step away from the man.

"Which is one reason you're leaving. She's *your* mother and not mine. I can take care of myself."

"Sure doesn't look like it."

Patric tried to focus on the boy's shadow. He stared at his small frame. Big punch in a small package. He might be young, but was brave beyond his years. Patric heard it in his voice. It had taken very little time to overcome his initial shock. As little as it had taken his mother.

"You've got a smart mouth for a little boy."

Silently, Patric acknowledged the boy's attempts at being a man. He wished he could have done the same at that age. Deciding not to encourage the boy's bravado, Patric crossed his arms across his chest. Did he look intimidating enough?

"I'm not little. I'm eight. I'm also the man of the family."

"So I gather. Where's your father?"

"None of your business."

"I asked you a question!" Patric snapped.

"Out of our lives," Callie answered sharply.

Patric turned toward the angry voice. Her shadow looked small in the frame of the door.

"I'm Cameron's mother and I'm all he needs. We don't need to live in a place like this with a man like you, that's for sure. We'll be out within the hour."

He shook his head and laughed softly. "You're going? Just like that? No arguments? I took you for more of a fighter."

Patric took a step and sat in the chair by the window. The sunlight shining in the floor-to-ceiling window had warmed the leather. He held back the sigh the comfort had summoned.

"I'm not interested in your opinions, or any games you might be trying to play."

"I was just wondering why is this job so important to you? Don't I have a right to know a bit more about you, if you plan on living in my home?"

"I have an eight year old son and I'm between homes. I need the roof over our heads, and I need the money."

"Why here?"

"Why not?"

"I have no patience for meddlesome busy-bodies, and

I have even less for children. I've been alone for some time now and I like it that way."

"Fine, then, we'll go." She paused before she spoke again. "I'm sorry I wasted your time. I hope you find whatever it is you think you're not looking for. Let's go, Cameron."

"You're a mean man, and I'm glad we're leaving." Cameron slammed the study door.

"I knew you'd quit," he shouted to the empty room. "Everyone quits on me."

The door burst open and anger filled the room. "I didn't quit, you fired me!"

He sensed her standing directly in front of him. "And is it any wonder everyone leaves you? You have a pretty crappy attitude."

"Try being blind and see how *your* attitude is."

"Try being a single mother without a penny who can't keep a damned job or home because no one wants children or pets." Callie leaned closer and the warmth of her breath brushed across his face. "I won't let anyone abuse me ever again. I've put up with it for far too long, and I deserve better."

Before he could ask what she meant, she left, slamming the door behind her.

Patric sat alone and waited for the sounds of the young boy to interrupt him. *Silence*. He stood up and made his way to the door. Pressing his ear against it he listened. *Silence*. How could two people move about without making any sounds at all? He leaned down when the small kitten rubbed against his leg. Picking the animal up, he thought for a brief moment how nice it would be to have a pet of his own. "Maybe she'll forget you."

A sharp knock on the door startled him. "Mr. LeClerc, I think my kitten is in your study."

He stepped away from the door and held the kitten against his cheek for a moment before he answered. "I have it." The hinges on the door squeaked and he waited for her shadow to come into view. He forced his eyes to focus, straining for a clearer image. He succeeded only in giving himself a headache.

"I'm sorry she got in here. At least now you won't have to be annoyed by it any more."

"Miss—Carpenter, I have to admit, I'm sorry to see you don't have the spunk it takes to succeed at working for me."

Callie almost choked. "I beg your pardon?"

"I may live alone and be out of touch with the changing world, but I learned at an early age that in order to succeed, one must have the strength to continue, even in the face of the unknown."

Callie couldn't believe her ears. He couldn't be challenging her. *Could he?* "I'm not sure I'm understanding you."

"Obviously. How do you expect to be a good nurse if you give up so easily?"

"I don't suppose it is any of your business, but I'm already a good nurse. A damn good nurse."

"Hmph. So, in nursing school now they teach you all to be quitters?"

"I'm not quitting. You—"

"I'm starving, and I would think if you cared about your job and your patient, you would feed him. Unless of course you really would rather quit." He arched his brow, a challenge to be sure.

Somehow she managed to keep her temper. "*If you*

think—never mind. I'll have your lunch ready in fifteen minutes."

Callie walked out of the room, quietly closing the door on her way out.

Cameron's alert hazel eyes flashed with concern as his mother came out of the room without the kitten. "Mom, where are we going to live?"

"Right here. Mr. LeClerc and I have reached an—understanding." *Of sorts.*

She considered going back in after Mardi, but couldn't erase the image of her boss holding the small kitten against his chest, he'd looked almost human. Almost.

"Does that mean I don't have to pack again?"

Callie rubbed her thumb across her son's cheek. "For now, sweetie. Who knows what he'll want five minutes from now." She nodded toward the study door. "That man has no clue what he wants."

She left her son standing in the hallway and made her way to the kitchen. She went to work slicing fruit and cheese. She took several of the cheese slices and slapped them between two slices of bread and grilled it. When she'd finished making the second sandwich, she turned the gas burner off and carried the tray into the dining room. She'd set the last plate on the table when the intercom crackled.

"I'll eat in the study."

She leaned against the table and sighed. "That man must have radar." She packed the tray back up and headed down the hallway. When she got to the door she considered knocking, but walked in instead. He wasn't there. He'd probably called from somewhere else in the house to torment her. Sensing his nearness, she spoke. "I left it on the table by the window. The sunlight will do you good." She scanned the room and left.

An hour later, she returned to the study and found the tray empty. Not so much as a crumb remained. At least he had a healthy appetite. Maybe a few good meals would improve his attitude. *Not likely,* she decided.

Callie made it through the rest of the day without having to face her boss again. But that was not to say that she had any peace. Several times throughout the afternoon he bellowed from afar. She considered taking the batteries out of all the intercoms to get some peace, but fought the urge.

She scrubbed the kitchen from top to bottom, and then helped Cameron settle into the room she had been told would be hers. She wasn't sure how long they were going to stay, but she refused to live in squalor if she could help it. She took down the grimy curtains and opened the shutters wide, letting the sunlight pour into the room as she and her son scoured the furniture, removing anything that looked valuable to the safety of Patric's study so Mardi would not be blamed for any damage.

Then they unpacked their meager possessions, and set to work in the adjoining bathroom. She made a hearty supper of chili and baked potatoes for all three of them, with a ready-made strawberry shortcake for dessert, and then set about finishing their room.

She hugged Cameron to her. "Thanks for all your help. It's not so bad now, is it?"

"Not too bad at all. But man, am I tired."

"Me too. I'm just going to check on a few more things downstairs. You get into your pjs, and into bed, and I'll see you in the morning."

""Okay, Mom. Goodnight."

"Goodnight, Cameron. Love you. Oh, and don't forget to brush your teeth."

A little before midnight Callie dropped into bed, exhausted. She fell asleep dreading the task ahead of her. She might have sorted out her own living arrangements, but after breakfast she'd have to get to work on the rest of the house. It would take her a month of Sundays to get all the grime and cobwebs down from the walls and ceilings. She didn't even want to think about the furniture and all the small figurines sitting around. This wasn't at all what she'd expected after years of nursing school. But there was no help for it. It had to be done. She was not going to be like all the other lazy employees who had just left Patric LeClerc to live in dirt.

As she drifted off to sleep, Mardi crawled up onto her bed and snuggled against her. She opened her eyes long enough to say goodnight, before falling into a sound slumber.

"Miss Carpenter, I'll assume you don't work on a schedule."

Callie jerked awake at the sound of his voice. Lying there for a minute, she wondered if she would ever get used to the blasted intercoms. The clock on her nightstand read 7:30 am. She had set it so she could be up by eight to get his breakfast ready.

"I'll be right down, Mr. LeClerc."

She stumbled out of bed, stepped on Mardi's tail, and whacked her knee on the nightstand. "Well, good morning to me."

"Morning, mom."

"Morning, sweetie. You stay in bed. I'm just going down for a little while, then we can do some stuff together later. He can't expect me to work al the time I"m here, now can he."

She pulled on a T-shirt and a pair of cut-offs, and headed down stairs. The hardwood floors scraped against her bare feet, and she made a mental note to find some slippers.

It took less than fifteen minutes to fix his eggs and ham slices. She set them on the table and went back to the kitchen. She pressed the "all" button and announced breakfast in the dining room.

"I'll be out in the storage house if you need me." Without waiting for his response she left the house.

CHAPTER THREE

Patric ate the tasty breakfast so fast he thought he might explode. He admitted to himself that though he might not like having Callie here, if he had to endure it, at least he'd get decent food. None of the other twits had bothered preparing a decent meal. Being blind didn't make him an idiot. He knew most of them had lived high off the hog on his money, while he had eaten next to nothing.

Patric heard a rustling behind him and froze. "Don't lurk around in the shadows. What do you want?"

Cameron cleared his throat. "I'm looking for my mom."

"Well, I haven't seen her."

Cameron laughed out loud.

"What's so funny?"

"I know you haven't seen her. You're blind."

Patric fought back the laugh bubbling up in his throat. "Wise guy." He turned toward the sounds and stared at the shadow. "What makes you think I know where your mother is?"

"I don't think. I came to find her and I found you instead. Mom said not to bother you, but I didn't know you were in here."

"Well, your mother is out in the storage shed."

"Thanks."

Callie looked up as her son lumbered into the musty building. "Hi, sport. I'll get you some breakfast in a minute. I still have to get used to getting up so early."

"I saw the boss."

"Don't call him that. His name is Mr. LeClerc." Callie stopped rummaging through the trunk and looked up at Cameron. "Where did you see him? Cameron, I told you not to bother him."

"I didn't. I was looking for you and I saw him in the big room where he eats."

"He's in the dining room? He can't still be eating."

"His plate was empty." Cameron leaned over and pulled an old hat out of the trunk. "Cool."

"Put that back. It doesn't belong to us."

"Mom, is it okay if I go out and look at the woods?"

Callie stopped. "Absolutely not. You are not to go anywhere near the woods. You could get lost."

"I won't get lost."

"I know, because you won't go into the woods alone. Understood?"

"Yes." He kicked at some loose gravel and mumbled something she didn't hear well enough to understand. "Well, then I'm going to go and play on the front steps."

"Be careful." Callie went directly to the dining room and cleared up the breakfast dishes. Once she'd washed everything and decided on the lunch menu, she headed to the front rooms to begin her cleaning.

Once she'd used all the dust rags she had found in the storage room, she gathered them up and took them to the laundry room. She looked at the pile of clothes and her blood boiled. What on earth was he wearing these days? She sorted the whole mountain into several piles, dark, permanent press, and whites, and tossed several pairs of jeans into the washer and started the cycle. The musty odor in the laundry made her gag, and she went in search of disinfectant spray.

While the first load of laundry ran, she made lunch and set it on the table. After she'd announced lunch, she waited in the dining room for him to come. Finally, she gave up and went back to work. Several times she shooed Mardi out of her cleaning bucket, and once she nearly shut the kitten in the dryer.

With three baskets of laundry to put away she headed upstairs. She opened door after door, looking for the master bedroom. Tired of carrying her load, she set them down and followed the sound of clinking. She stopped outside the door and stared into the room. Twice the size of the others, it loomed in front of her. Inside she saw him, sprawled out on his back with a weight bar across his chest. His pale gold skin glistened with beads of sweat as he lifted and lowered the bar.

With each repetition, he exhaled slowly, pulling from within himself the strength to do it again. She watched the muscles in his arms flex and bulge with the strain of the weights. *Glorious* was the only word she could come up with to describe him. Even the unhealthy pallor of his skin didn't detract from his looks. He had a body that should have been displayed in a museum with the classical sculptures, hard and honed to near perfection. The only detail which marred the impression was his dark and scraggly hair, which hung over the side of the bench. She longed to loosen the tangles and run her fingers through it. Combed out, it would be beautiful.

Startled at that thought, and feeling like a peeping Tom, Callie stepped back away from the door. She held perfectly still when the clanking of the bar stopped. It wasn't until he resumed his workout she dared leave. She picked up the baskets and hurried to the other end of the hallway.

Cameron held the handful of wild roses and watched the man pull himself up over the bar again and again. He had muscles bigger than any he'd ever seen before. Boy, would he love to have muscles that big. Then he could beat up anyone who called him a sissy. He leaned against the wall, but didn't notice its creaking.

The giant stopped his workout and looked toward him. Cameron froze. The man's hair looked wet, and he reminded Cameron of a bear. Cameron stared into the silver eyes, unable to look away.

"I told you to stay the hell out of my wing."

Cameron gulped.

"I knew I should have made you leave. You and that damn kid of yours have no business being here. Get the hell out of here, and if you step foot on this side of the house again, I'll throw you out myself."

Cameron turned around and ran down the hall as fast as his legs would carry him. He tripped over the carpet and slid down the hallway. He took a quick glance over his shoulder expecting to see the giant chasing after him. When he saw no one, he took a second to breathe before getting up and running down the stairs. Cameron jerked open the kitchen door and bolted out toward the storage building.

Callie came out of the spare room when she heard the door downstairs slam. A split second, later she heard the roar.

"This is my house and I swear I won't let you, or your brood of misfits invade my life and turn it upside down."

Callie walked calmly toward the thundering voice,

wondering what had set him off this time. She'd never known anyone so determined to make a mountain out of every little molehill. "Is something wrong, Mr. LeClerc?"

"You know damn good and well something's wrong. If you want to see a freak show, go into town and visit the damn circus. I told you when you got here that this side of the house is off limits. That includes lurking around in corners and spying on me. I expect—no, I *demand* my privacy, and if you can't stick to my guidelines you can get the hell out now."

Callie took a deep breath before responding. "Maybe you could tell me what it is I've supposedly done."

"I know you were just standing outside my room watching me. Don't bother denying it, I heard you running down the hall."

"I'm sorry to tell you, but I've been right here. I'm putting away your clean clothes." Callie gestured toward the bedroom, then remembered he couldn't see her.

"I heard you run away, so give it up."

"Why would I run away? Cameron!" Callie stepped toward him and her motherly instincts kicked in. "What have you done to my son?"

"What have *I* done?" He paused. "You weren't outside my room?"

"I told you I wasn't. Maybe you should try listening to someone else once in a while instead of bellowing at the top of your lungs."

"I assumed it was you." Patric shifted his weight from one foot to the other.

"What made you assume it was me?"

"I smelled—"

"Oh great, I spend the entire day cleaning your filthy house and now you insult me by telling me I stink. That's

45

rich."

"I didn't say you—"

"Never mind. I have to find my son, and if you harmed one hair on his head, I swear I'll—"

"I didn't touch him. I would never—"

Her bare feet padded down the hall away from him. She'd actually walked off and left him talking to himself. Damn her. Who did she think she was?

Callie searched every room on all three floors. After nearly two hours of searching, she began to panic. She decided to check the grounds before she called the police. She made it as far as the corner of the storage building when she heard a crash.

Instinct told her she'd found her son, it also made her fear he'd been hurt. She opened the door and flicked the light switch. "Cameron, it's Mom. Are you in here?"

The response came in the form of a soft sniffle. She stepped further into the room and searched for her son. She saw the toe of his shoe sticking out from under the cloth-covered table.

"Honey, I know Mr. LeClerc scared you, but it's okay now."

"Nuh uh. He said he'd throw us out into the street. He sweared at me and yelled really loud." He sniffled again.

"I know, sweetie, but he didn't mean it."

"Yes he did."

Callie stuck her hand under the cloth for him to hold. "Maybe you scared him too."

Cameron put his little hand in hers and she squeezed it. "How could I scare someone as big as him?"

"Honey, he can't see you. If he didn't hear you walk

up, you might have startled him." Callie tugged on his hand and he reluctantly crawled out from under the table. "Oh look at your face. You have dirt and spider webs all over you."

"This place is dirty."

"You shouldn't have come out here alone. I was looking all over for you."

"I'm hiding." Cameron curled up in her lap and wrapped his arms around her neck. "You won't let him get me, will you?"

Callie hugged him close and kissed the soft brown hair covering his head. "Were you hiding from me too?"

"No, just him. I like it here, but I don't like him."

"Well, I'm going to make sure he doesn't yell at you anymore. What do you say we go back in the house and I'll find you a snack?"

"'Kay."

Once she had Cameron settled in their room, she went in search of her employer. "Mr. LeClerc, I need to talk to you."

"I thought we established I wasn't deaf."

Callie stepped into the study and glared in his direction. He'd pulled the drapes and the only light in the room came from the hallway. "You may not be deaf, but you are by far the most insensitive man I have ever met."

"And your point is?"

"My point is, that you will never again yell, or swear at my son. If you so much as look at him cross—if you go near him, I'll deal with you in my own way."

Patric stood, but didn't move. "First of all, I didn't know it was the kid. I thought it was you spying on me."

"What right do you have to yell at me?" Callie snapped. "Why do you always have to yell?"

"I don't have to. I choose to."

"Well, that makes it all right, then, does it?" Callie marveled at his audacity. The man didn't care who he offended and went out of his way to be a pain in the—

She tried to remain calm, however. "Mr. LeClerc, Patric, I understand that this couldn't have been easy for you. I also think you should understand that my life hasn't been easy either."

Patric moved toward her, but she held her ground. "Maybe if we try to talk to each other…."

"Talk? As if that will solve anything. You don't understand anything about me, or my life. You have no clue what it's like to be blind. To know there is so much out there and you're missing it. I had my sight and was robbed of it because my father—"

"What?"

He shook his head.

"What about your father?"

Callie desperately wanted to know what had caused his blindness, but the set determination in his face told her she wouldn't find out now. Maybe she didn't need to know. Knowing too much about him might make it harder to leave. But she wasn't so sure she wanted to leave.

"All right then, don't tell me about yourself. I am here to talk about me anyway. Me and my family. Do you think it's been easy for me? Or for Cameron? He's been moved three times in less than a year, and has lost his father. My ex abandoned us, left us with nothing. So I have been doing everything I can to make ends meet. Now I find a place that I think can be a home for him, and a good job with the only decent prospect of money we've had in years, and he has some strange man shouting at him for God knows what. He's a child and you are a grown man, but at this moment, I'm having a hard time distinguishing between the two."

Patric flinched at her words. Her anger swarmed around her, and reminded him of how he'd felt when his father had come after him. He'd sworn no one would ever treat him like that again. In his house they would abide by his rules. If not for his damn over-protective estate executor, he wouldn't tolerate this damn nurse business one more minute.

"Very well then. You've made yourself clear. I can see you have had a hard time. But this is my home, and I make the rules. So I am telling you now, to make sure that there will be no questions in the future, you'll keep your child, and yourself away from my wing from now on."

"No, I'll make sure Cameron stays as far away from you as possible, but I need to get into those rooms to clean them and get some of this mess put away."

"I said—"

"I heard you, but I can't agree to that. I am a nure. I hae to be concerned for your health. This place is so dirty it is close to being condemned and I can't in good conscience leave it this way. Whether or not I stay here, doesn't matter, but while I am here, I'll be cleaning everything. Including *your* side of the house."

Patric waited for her to go, but she didn't.

In the end he shrugged. "Just stay out of my way." He reached out for the table in front of him and silently counted his steps to the door. He reached for the knob.

"It's open."

"I know."

Patric stepped into the hallway and cursed the effect

she had on his senses. She'd thrown his usual regimented life into total chaos and he was getting damned tired of walking into walls. Since Callie's arrival, he'd miscounted steps, he'd tripped, and he set things on tables that weren't where he thought they were. Maybe he should just can her and get back to his own life. *But what about the kid?*

Small feet stopped at the landing of the stairs. He raised his head and waited. Patric had no idea what he was waiting for.

"Sorry, I'll go back up 'til you pass."

Cameron's voice had lost some of its spunk. In fact, he sounded terrified. Patric's insides shrunk up at the thought of having scared the boy. His life hadn't been a picnic, but it wasn't the kid's fault, and he wasn't really a bad kid after all. "Hold on there."

"No, mom says to stay out of your way." Cameron's feet shuffled on the carpeted stairs.

"I know what she told you, but it's my house."

"Yeah, so?"

A hint of a spark crept back into his little voice and Patric smiled, but only on the inside. "I've got something to say, and I want you to hear it from me."

"Are you gonna kick us out?"

"No, what makes you think that?"

"You said you were gonna."

Patric had to hand it to the kid, he was a smart one. Maybe too smart. Patric thought about it for a minute and reached a new conclusion. "Maybe I was wrong."

"Yeah?"

"Maybe I came out here to say I'm sorry."

"Yeah?"

"Hey, kid, can you say anything but yeah?"

Cameron giggled. "Yeah?"

"Cute, kid. I really am sorry. I didn't know it was you, or I wouldn't have yelled at you like that."

"You shouldn't yell at anyone. Mom says it's rude."

"Your mom talks a lot." Patric closed his eyes and thought of her sweet voice, the same voice that only moments earlier had cut him to the quick.

Callie stepped up behind him as he spoke.

Cameron saw her and swallowed hard. "Yeah, but she's always right."

"Cameron, lets go for a walk. We need to have a little talk." Callie stepped past Patric and reached up for her son's hand as he bolted down the stairs. As Cameron brushed past Patric she heard the man whisper something.

"Yeah, a lot."

Cameron giggled, but when she asked what her boss had said, she got a shrug of the shoulders and an uninterested brush off.

"I need to ask you something, Cam. And you can be totally honest with me."

"'Kay."

"Do you want to leave here? I know Mr. LeClerc yelled and scared you, and that's okay. If this is too scary for you, mom can find another job."

"Mom, I don't care. He is scary, but I don't want you to be sad anymore. Daddy made you sad and when we went away you stopped being scared. So, I just don't want you to be scared any more."

"Let's go back inside, I need to take care of something."

Since it was already getting late, Callie cleaned her son up, tucked Cameron into bed and went back down to make supper for Patric. Afterwards, she cleaned up the supper dishes. She hated having to clean the kitchen and dining room for one meal, but she consoled herself with the thought that it wouldn't be for too much longer.

When she was finished with her chores, she closed the kitchen door, and went to the front porch. A light drizzle of rain fell from the dark sky. She sat on the swing and watched the gray clouds scurry across the darkening evening sky. They reminded her of the way her life had been going. Nothing stayed the same. Every time she thought things would clear up and the sun would come out, it would start to rain again. Patric LeClerc had become the biggest rain cloud in her life.

"He's a good boy."

Callie jumped at the sound of his voice. She'd been so lost in her thoughts she hadn't heard him step onto the porch. She'd always thought blind people would be loud and clumsy. He prowled around like a panther, a caged and very dangerous beast. The sad part being that he'd built his own cage, and kept himself locked inside.

"I know. In spite of everything, he's done so well."

"He's lucky to have a mother like you. I knew from the beginning you were different."

Callie stared at him. He stood above her, his face pointed toward the sky. His matted hair moved with the wind from the storm. She noticed he'd trimmed his beard, or tried to. She wanted to reach up and touch the odd-length whiskers, but his words stopped her.

"I don't know what I'm supposed to do." He inched his foot forward. "The last thing I need is an entire family under foot."

When his foot moved dangerously close to the edge of the step, she touched his leg. "What do you mean?"

"I've got it," he insisted, pushing her hand away.

Callie moved to stand, but he sat instead. "Have it your own way, then. You always seem to."

As they sat side by side silently, Callie's thought swirled in her head. She'd worked with numerous disabled people. None of them had been like Patric. This man's attempts at independence bordered on annoying. He used his blindness as a weapon and she couldn't honestly admit, even to herself, that she was willing to be a victim to the kind of abuse that he had shorn himself capable of dishing out. The money, the offer of a home, they were tempting, all right, but there was self-respect too. And safety. With Patric LeClerc so changeable and moody all the time, just as her ex had been, neither of them could ever feel safe. No, it was never going to work. Better to cut her losses now, and go. She took a deep breath. Callie knew what she had to do. "I'm giving my notice, Mr. LeClerc."

"You can't do that!" he practically bellowed.

Callie turned on him, astonished. He had been doing nothing but trying to get rid of them. Now he was telling her to stay? It made no sense.... "That reaction of yours is exactly why I have to go. I can't have my son being raised in a house with all this anger and hostility. We left one situation like that. I am not walking right back into another."

She watched Patric's expression change from anger to pain. His features relaxed and grew haunted by something she was ignorant of.

"Can you blame me for being angry?" He lowered his head and let it rest on his arms. "I've never known anything but anger."

"So the rest of the world has to suffer along with you?

My son has done nothing to you, and yet your tone of voice and language scared the devil out of him."

Callie stood and stepped out into the rain. The cool drops of rain slipped down her face and soothed her own anger.

"I didn't do it on purpose."

"All the more reason for us to leave. You have absolutely no control over your emotions, and I can't take the risk of you flying off the handle again." She stepped up in front of him and watched him.

"Why are you staring at me?" He leaned forward and Callie stepped back. "Before you ask, I just knew."

"What's made you so angry?"

"It's not important. Besides, it isn't really any of your business."

Callie frowned and turned back into the rain. How could anyone change moods so quickly? But she knew the answer to that. There was no reason. Her husband had never had any reason to be brutally angry, and yet he always had been. "Well, I've tired to clear the air with you, but if you are not going to talk with me, ust bark orders, there is nothing more to be said. I'll just go up and turn in now. I'll be up first thin in the morning to cook your breakfast, and when I get into town, I'll tell them to make arrangements for a new nurse to come out as soon as possible."

Patric stood up quickly. "Did it ever occur to you I might not want a new nurse?" He moved his foot and stumbled forward.

Callie saw him falling, but could do nothing to stop him, so she put herself between him and the ground. He slammed into her, and pain shot through her as they both hit the ground.

"Son of a—"

"Are you all right?"

Callie pulled herself out from under him, ignoring the thrilling sensations that had coursed through her as his lean hard frame had pinned her to the ground, and she knelt beside him. "Patric?"

"I'm fine, for a man who just fell down steps for the first time in ten years." He sat up and rubbed his knee. "I fell down these steps once when I was seven. My father called me a disgrace because I couldn't walk like a man. I was only seven."

"Accidents happen."

Patric's heart skipped. "Yeah, they happened a lot around my father."

"So how did you end up losing your eyesight?" Callie expected a blast of anger, but only sadness lingered in his expression. Soft lines dipped low over his brow and she longed to brush them away with her fingertips. "You don't have to tell me if you don't want to. It doesn't really matter."

His head shot up and he turned to face her. A single tear slipped down his cheek before his guard came up again and he lit into her. "You're right. It doesn't matter. It never has and it never will. I've survived on my own for this long, and I don't need you or anyone else to keep on doing it."

"That's not what I meant. I just didn't want you to think you had to tell me. I'm not here because of you. I'm here because of Cameron and me. I need to earn a living and I need a roof over our heads. Your roof is as good as any."

He thrust his fingers into his hair and cringed when they caught in the tangled mess. Callie reached up and brushed a few stray locks away from his forehead. He stopped when her fingers brushed against his skin. He took her hand in his and held it briefly. Something in the set of his jaw changed and he snatched his hand away. Callie recognized the attack of insecurity.

Something in this man's past had wounded him badly, and she didn't know if she had the strength, or desire to find out what it was and fix it.

"So, basically you're using me to get what you want?"

Callie considered slapping him, but didn't see any point. His voice dripped with sarcasm and nothing would change him or the way he saw things. "I'm doing what I have to do to survive, so long as I can do it honestly and keep my self-respect, and if that means working here, then I'll do it."

"I thought you were quitting. Would it be too much to ask you to make up your damn mind?"

In her entire life she'd never been so annoyed with one person as she was with this man. Not even Jason. "Would it be too much to ask you to keep a civil tongue in your head and not swear at me, or my child?"

"You stay and I'll stop swearing."

"One more thing."

Callie reached out toward him and he pulled away from her. "Don't."

"I don't think you are in any position to make demands. Do you?"

Callie smiled. "What have I got to lose?" She brushed the matted hair back and let her hand rest against his head. "I want you to let me give you a shave and a haircut."

"What the hell for? It doesn't make a damn bit of difference what I look like and why in the hell—"

"Never mind. I'll be tomorrow morning."

"What the he—" he paused and raised his head. "Oh."

For a moment Patric considered laughing out loud, but the tightening in his mid-section silenced him. He hadn't cared how he looked in a long time. Too long. Something about the sound of Callie Carpenter's voice made him care. He'd sensed something different in her the first time they'd met. He didn't need sight to see what she held inside. Reality washed over him and he cursed himself for a fool. No one with her sensitivity would ever consider being tied down to someone like him. A woman with her spark and zest for life needed a whole man, not an invalid.

"What about your hair? It's my final offer. If you agree, I promise not to quit again, at least not until the end of the month, when I can be really sure that you will be able to manage on your own. ."

Patric thought about refusing, but the thought of her velvety soft, slender fingers in his hair and touching his face would be worth a little bit of discomfort and wasted time. "If that's what it'll take to get some peace, then you can have one afternoon to make me look respectable."

"You make it sound like a fate worse than death. Besides, I never said you didn't look respectable."

"Oh, and I can tell you are totally smitten with my rugged good looks."

Where had that come from? What did it matter what she thought? It didn't. Patric tried to remember what he looked like. He recalled the last time he'd seen himself, his own terrified reflection in the rear-view mirror of his father's car, just before the drunken fool had driven it into a ravine. The last vision he had was of the blood on his mother's face as she had slipped into a coma, and had soon after died.

"So I will take that as an agreement that I can stay. So, tomorrow, I'm going to cook you breakfast, spend the morning with Cameron, and then I'll come get you in the afternoon and we'll see what we can do about your rugged good looks as you call them."

"So, does this mean you're staying?"

"As long as you keep your end of the bargain, we'll stay. I just need to know my son will be safe."

Patric wanted to be insulted by the insinuation that he would ever do anything to harm a child, but he couldn't. For all she knew he was as horrible a monster as he looked. He imagined jagged scars lining his face and chest, red swollen rims around the sockets of his eyes and his hair. He'd tried every day for a year to comb the mess, but had given up after a while.

He imagined bald patches in his beard where the scars refused to let the hair grow. No, he couldn't blame her at all.

"Cameron will be fine. You have my word on it."

Patric listened to her shifting in front of him. She moved hesitantly. What was she unsure of? Him? He hated the thought of frightening her as much as her son.

"Do I frighten you?" he asked, not wanting to know the answer.

"Well, not anymore." Callie stopped moving.

He stood up and slid his foot back against the next higher step. Carefully he made his way to the front door and pushed it open.

"Maybe you should be scared," Patric said quietly. Then he disappeared.

Callie let out the breath she'd been holding. *He's so*

wrong. Her heart made it perfectly clear she had nothing to fear from him. *Damned heart.* She could try and kid herself into thinking it was the training she'd had in nursing school, but it was more. Sometimes when she saw him sitting alone she looked at his eyes, not quite vacant, but definitely empty. What would it take to fill the emptiness inside him? Or inside her for that matter?

CHAPTER FOUR

After fixing lunch the next day, Callie fell onto her bed, exhausted. Cameron and she had gone outside investigating. She'd forgotten how much energy her son could store up. She fed Patric his breakfast, done some chores, and then gone on an expedition with Cameron. They'd seen every inch of the estate that was not wooded. She'd firmly refused to let him go into the densely forested area.

Then she had come back to prepare some food for all of them, and washed the dishes, managing to squeeze in three more loads of washing and drying that day. With Cameron tucked nicely in their room with crayons, a pad of paper, and a stack of coloring books, she could rest for a while.

"Miss Carpenter, I don't have all day. Are you coming to help me or not?"

"Blasted intercom." Callie lifted herself off the bed and stabbed her finger against the "speak" button. "And where is it you plan on going?"

"This was your idea."

She sighed and rested her head against the wall. "Coming," *your highness,* she added under her breath.

With what little energy she had left, Callie went down over to his wing. She listened for signs of movement, and heard them in the master bedroom. She stepped up to the door and lifted her hand to knock.

"Come in, Miss Carpenter."

Callie stepped into the room. "What's different?" She'd been in his room several times, putting away clean laundry, but had not yet made any effort to really clean it up. That was what was different. He had, since last night. The laundry she hadn't got to put away was nowhere to be seen, and he'd pulled the quilt up over the bed.

"Can we get this over with?" he grumbled.

Callie faced him, surprised. Though he sounded impatient, it wasn't the kind of annoyance she'd grown used to hearing in his tone. She looked at him and realized he'd put on clean clothes. Her heart raced with understanding. He'd cleaned up for her. "I guess I should start by—I mean you should—your hair needs to be washed." Callie didn't want to step on his independent toes, but he obviously had a problem doing it himself.

She watched him move into the bathroom and followed. When she stepped in behind him, he reached for the sink faucet and turned the water on. The fabric of his shirt pulled against his back as he yanked a towel off the shelf. A second towel slipped off the wire rack and Callie caught it. Her body pressed against his side and they both froze. "Sorry."

"Let's just do it." The low growl of his voice caught her off guard. It wasn't anger she heard, but something more unsettled.

Her mind raced, but she blocked out the images the contact with his hard masculine body had conjured up. Without speaking, Patric leaned down and put his head under the water. She took a cup from the counter and filled it. As the stream of water rolled down his neck, he shivered, and Callie remembered all the times her mother had washed her hair. She loved the way the water trickled down around her ears and chills rushed along the base of her skull. It always relaxed her. Maybe washing Patric's hair would have the same effect on him. Nobody needed to relax more than he did. She dipped her fingers into his hair and gently massaged his scalp.

Patric relaxed against the feel of her hands in his hair. Her fingertips manipulated and rubbed against the mats of hair he'd left untended for so long. The fragrance of shampoo wafted around him as she scrubbed and scratched at his scalp with her nails. Incredible, simply incredible. He'd never known such ecstasy in all of his life. He wondered how something so basic could have such an affect on him.

As the thought occurred to him, she leaned across his back and her breast brushed against him. The hardness of her nipples made his legs go weak.

"Are you almost finished? I'm getting a cramp." If only it were something so simple as a cramp. He had a throbbing in his jeans like he'd never known.

"Almost. Look at it this way. Once we do this you shouldn't have any problems for a while. We can keep it brushed out and it won't get to be such a—"

"Mess?"

"I'm sorry, Mr. LeClerc. I didn't mean to be rude."

"You're not, and for Pete's sake, stop calling me Mr. LeClerc. I'm not my father."

He realized he'd shouted at her and lowered his voice. "My name is Patric and if you plan on hanging around, you might as well get over being so formal."

"Then you can call me Callie." She took the towel from him and wrapped it around his head.

Several drops of water rolled down his face and she caught them with her fingertips. The stubble from his beard scratched against her nails, and the vibration nearly knocked him down. She turned him around and he could see the shadow of her face. Without knowing why, he reached for her hair. The soft locks brushed against his hand and he closed his fingers around them.

Soft didn't begin to describe the texture and his mind struggled to form an image of the color. Maybe chocolate brown. Maybe he could ask her.

"It's murky brown."

"What is?" He spoke past the lump in his throat and hoped she couldn't tell.

"My hair. That's what my ex—husband called it last time I saw him. Murky brown."

Patric rubbed the hair between his fingers and twisted a few strands. He smelled the balsam shampoo she used, distinctly different from the dandruff shampoo she'd chosen to use on his hair. "I doubt he gave an accurate assessment. He is after all an ex."

"What does that have to do with anything?" She scrubbed the towel against his head and stepped away from him.

Her hair slipped from his grasp. His hands shook and he dropped them to his lap. "Well, who wouldn't want to be married to Florence Nightingale? I mean, you take great care of Cameron, and I can't imagine you as anything less than a doting wife."

"Your remarks are flattering, no matter how untrue. I haven't always been the model of domesticity. In fact—"

"I don't recall anyone having to be perfect to be a good wife."

"Only if you're married to Jason. It was part of the prenuptial I didn't read." Her voice drifted off.

A strange odor came out of nowhere and he tried to place it. Before he'd figured it out, her hands plunged into his hair and the smell grew stronger. She rubbed and massaged and his eyes drifted shut. "Mmm."

"I'm not sure how I'll get all the tangles out from underneath. The top layer is okay, but underneath—"

"Mmm." His head rolled forward and his mind went blank. Well, not totally blank. He had a very distinct image of the woman who'd managed to get into his hair. She stood before him under a full moon, a beautiful summer night. Off in the distance he heard the laughter of a child, no, children. His mind pushed for a clearer image, but the image grew misty and began to fade. "No."

"Patric, did I hurt you? I'm sorry." Her hands settled on his shoulders and he leaned into her grasp.

"No, I'm fine. My head is harder than that." He shifted in his seat. *Much harder.*

She resumed her combing. The longer she worked on his hair, the more relaxed he grew. The soft tugging lulled him to a place he hadn't been in a very long time. A place with no dark images, no screaming and no grating metal. Soothing images surrounded him and the low echoes of relaxation pulled him deeper.

His mother's smiling face wavered in his mind. Her lips moved, but no sound came out. Then he felt the words. "Patric, you deserve to be happy. I need you to be happy for us. Please, Paddy, don't give up the way I did. You have the—"

Then the words faded and the face disappeared. His clenched his eyes tighter and prayed for her face to come back. *Please mama, don't leave me again. I don't know how to do this. I can't do this.*

"Patric." The concerned edge to the voice snapped

him back to reality. "Tell me what's wrong. You're scaring me." Her velvety hands held his face and her breath washed over him.

"Patric?"

"I'm sorry, Miss Carpenter, my mind seems to be inclined to wander off without me. I think it's time we finish this up. I have things to do." He held out his hand and snapped his fingers. "The comb." He paused. "Please."

Callie stood up and took a step away from him. One minute he'd been sighing and the next, back to growling. She'd never understand how his moods could change so quickly and for no good reason. "I'm sorry I took so long, but I got it all combed out. If you keep at it every—"

"I know how to comb my hair, thank you."

"Of course you do. I only meant—"

"That'll be all." He sat silent.

Finally, Callie turned and walked out of the room. She looked back in time to see him rest his head in his hands. She considered going back in, but decided she was in no mood to be kicked again. "If you're so desperate to be alone, then far be it from me to interfere with your pity party."

She marched down the hall and into the kitchen where she set about banging every pot and cabinet door she could. "Infuriating, self-centered, mean-spirited tyrant."

The silver spatula clinked into the stainless steel sink. "Spiders can grow in your hair for all I care."

Mardi wrapped around her feet and she lifted a socked toe to scratch his back. "He's a monster all right, Mardi. A big overgrown baby of a monster."

Meow.

She looked down at her confidant and smiled. "You always know the right thing to say, don't you?"

"Mom, can I go out for a walk?" Cameron stood in the kitchen doorway with his hands tucked in his jeans' pockets.

For nearly a week, he'd stayed upstairs, or been out walking the grounds. They'd had a long talk about Mr. LeClerc's need for privacy and peace. More than that, Callie needed to know he wouldn't be influenced by the man's bad attitude. If they remained separated there would be no problems. "Where are you planning on going? You must have already seen everything there is to see."

Her thoughts skipped to Patric. How much of his estate had he seen? She gathered he'd lived here as a child, but things could have changed while he was away. Had he actually seen it since his return, or the accident?

"Mom, can I?"

"I don't know, sweetie. I worry about you being out there alone."

"Aw, mom, I promised I would never go near the woods alone."

She loved her son and every mother had a right to worry, but she also knew he was a good boy and never lied or made promises he wouldn't keep. "All right, but don't go far."

"Okey dokey." Cameron turned and walked away. He smiled as he slipped up the stairs and headed to the right. He glanced back to make sure he wasn't being watched before disappearing into the gloomy corridor. He knocked lightly on the door.

"What?"

"It's Cameron. I want to ask you something."

Cameron stuffed his hands in his pockets and looked around. Pictures hung on both sides of the hall. Ugly pictures with weird animals and dark colors. One in particular caught his attention and he wandered over to get a good look at it. A two—headed dragon of some sort swooped down to pick up a girl from a field. Blood dripped from its mouth. Cameron stared at the picture for a few minutes, until he was sure the monster was staring at him. He decided he hated it and went back to the door.

"Are you coming in or not?" the voice grumbled from inside the room.

"As soon as you tell me to."

"Well, why bother to wait, I told you not to come into this part of the house and here you are, so why wait for permission?"

"Can I, or not?"

"Come in for—goodness sake."

Cameron strolled into the room and looked around. "Wow." He noticed all the piles of dirty laundry laying around and then he spotted the small door next to the dressing room. "What's this?"

"Well, if I could see, I would probably have a better chance of telling you."

Cameron rolled his eyes as he walked across the room. "It's a little door." He pulled the handle out and peered down into the chute. "It looks like it goes down a long way."

Patric sighed. A damn laundry chute. Why in the hell hadn't anyone bothered to remind him about the chute? "What do you want kid?"

He stood up and waited for the boy to start talking. He could follow his voice and count the steps to the door. Then he could get some of this laundry out of his way, or, he thought, he could just ask Callie to come up and get it. Nope. She'd made it perfectly clear since the incident in the bathroom that she was only doing her job. Thoughts of her reminded him of the rose water perfume she wore and he missed the scent.

"I came up to get you. I thought maybe you would like to go for a walk with me. Mom said I should leave you alone, but she also said before that you are lonely, and if you are, then if you go for a walk with me, I can make you not lonely. Mom says it's nice—"

"Hey, kid." Patric was right, while the kid yammered on about lord knows what, he could have walked to China and back. "Anyone ever tell you that you talk too much?"

"Like my mom?"

"Yeah, kid. Like your mom."

"Well, it is kinda lonely out here. I don't have any other kids to play with or talk to, and mom is really busy trying to get the downstairs rooms all cleaned, and she said she was gonna paint, and I figured if—"

"She's gonna do what?" Patric headed toward the door, carefully counting his steps so he didn't knock anything over in front of the kid. He reached the door and stopped. "Why did you come to get me?"

"Well, mom said if anyone got in her way they were gonna have to help paint. So, I figured if we went out for a walk, neither one of us would have to help."

Patric tried to come up with a damn good reason to forbid her to paint, but couldn't. The simple truth was he didn't want to go outside. He hadn't been out of the house in nearly eight years. It wouldn't do anyone any good if he got out there and got lost. He'd be damned if he would sit in the middle of nowhere, lost, waiting to be rescued. No way.

"Come on, I found some really neat places and I wanna show 'em to you."

"Kid, aren't you forgetting? I can't see."

"Yeah, but I saw on television once where these people would go places and they would talk into tape players so blind people could see the pictures they were talking about. I could do that for you."

Patric reached out for the wall, then leaned against it. "So, you wanna make tapes for me?"

"No, silly, I want you to go along and I'll tell you about stuff when I see it. I could be like your dog. You know, one of those blind seeing dogs."

"A seeing-eye dog." Patric groaned. Obviously the kid was really hard up for someone to talk to if he was willing to be a guide dog. "I'll go as far as the back porch, but that's my limit."

Patric pushed the door open and held his hand out. "Let's go, before I change my mind."

Part way down the hall, Cameron grabbed his hand. Patric thought about pulling away, but the contact brought back memories of walking with his mother and he needed to be able to hold onto those memories, so he didn't let go.

The first rays of sunlight heated the sleeve of his shirt. How different it was from the way things felt at night. No moisture from the air dampened his skin, and no breeze blew around him. He listened to the birds and the bugs twittering off in the distance, not like the bullfrogs and crickets from the twilight. Cameron let go of his hand and he listened to the boy run down the steps.

"Are you coming?"

"No. I told you I'd only go as far as the porch." A lump formed in his throat as he listened to the rustling of the grass.

"What are you doing, kid?"

"Just playing with this thing."

Something close to panic raced through him and Patric tapped his toe forward, looking for the step. "Playing with what?"

"This bug thing. Come look—come here and I'll let you hold it."

Patric tried to dredge up even the smallest amount of enthusiasm about holding a bug thing. Lack of eyesight had a tendency to make one leery of things that crawl or fly, something about the advantage of surprise they had. "Er, no thanks."

But before he knew it, Cameron had his hand again and was dragging him across the yard. Several times he tripped over roots or clumps of dirt or grass, and each time Cameron stopped long enough for him to regain his footing before taking off again.

"We're almost there. Just a little farther." The excitement in the boys voice wrapped around him and in spite of his initial apprehension, Patric couldn't ignore his own curiosity.

As quickly as they'd started, they stopped. Patric nearly knocked the child down when he bumped into him. "Where are we?"

"We're by the—wait. Listen."

Patric held his breath and listened. At first he couldn't be sure, but then he recognized the sounds from his childhood. Fish jumping. His excitement grew as he took a reluctant step forward. "How far are we from the water?"

"If you take another step, you're gonna have to explain to mom why your shoe is wet." Cameron laughed and so did Patric.

"We don't want that. I don't need anything else to be in trouble for."

"Yeah, me neither."

The two of them spent the rest of the afternoon wading in the shallow water and splashing each other. Deciding it was time to get dried, they lay down in the tall grass and let the sun dry their clothes. It wouldn't do to go home soaked to the bone.

Callie heard the car pull up as she walked around the house. She'd gone out to look for Cameron, but had had no luck. She came around the house and ran straight into the chest of her ex—husband. "Jason, what are you doing out here?"

"I might ask you the same thing. What are you thinking, bringing my son out to this hell hole?"

"First of all, he's *my* son, and it's none of your business where we are." She shielded her eyes against the sun as she glared up at him. "What do you want?"

In his usual intimidating way he stepped forward. A year ago, she would have stepped back, but today she held her ground. Standing close enough to touch, she asked him again.

"I came to spend some time with my son."

"I don't think that's a good idea." Cold palpable fear raced through every fiber of her being. Nothing in the world could have prepared her for Jason's sudden interest in a son he'd never wanted or acknowledged.

"I have right to see my boy." He reached out and grazed her cheek with his thumb. "You know, Cal, you really oughta take better care of your skin. It feels like leather. You're looking kinda haggard. Let me take the boy off your hands for a while."

What little self-confidence she'd managed to maintain over the years slowly slipped away. How could a man she hadn't seen, or thought about in nearly a year, still have the power to leave her feeling worthless? "Jason, I'm doing fine without you, so just go away and leave Cameron and me alone."

His laugh echoed around her and sent shivers along her spine. The man had no heart, but then she already knew that. What she needed to know now was why he had tracked her down, and what he wanted with Cameron.

"Callie, I will spend time with my son, and nothing you can say or do will stop me."

"Jason, you don't even know him. You haven't seen him in almost two years and even when we were married you only looked at him if it were absolutely essential."

Her palms began to sweat and she wondered where Cameron was. She couldn't let Jason know she had no clue where her son had run off to. As if he'd read her mind, Cameron came running around the corner of the house. His brown hair was sticking straight up on end and he had dirt smeared all over his face.

"Mom, what are you—" He skidded to a halt and glared up at his father. Protectively, he stepped to his mother's side and reached for her hand. "What is he doing here?"

"Mind your mouth, boy. Is that any way to speak to your father?"

Cameron's small brown eyes narrowed as he glared up at the man he knew only as the bad man. He was the only person who'd ever made his mother cry. Then he thought about it. Nope, the boss had made her cry too.

But he wasn't really mean, just cranky because he was blind. But this mean man was different. Mean for no reason.

"Go away, we don't want you to be here. This is where we live now and you don't. Go away." Cameron tugged on his mother's hand and tried to lead her to the front porch.

Jason moved to physically block them.

"I'm not finished talking to your mother. You go on into the house, son, and we'll follow."

Cameron looked up toward the house, hoping to catch a glimpse of Mr. LeClerc. When he didn't see him, he held fast to his mother's hand. "You can't tell me what to do."

"I said go, boy. Don't sass me. Now git."

Callie pushed Cameron behind her and stepped up to confront the man she'd been so glad to divorce. Years of abuse and anger had held her prisoner and she would not allow her son to be tainted by those things.

"Don't you ever raise your voice to my son again, or I'll deal with you myself." She turned and pulled her son along behind her. She smiled when Cameron stuck his tongue out at his father.

"Callie, if you won't deal with me, we can take this back into court."

Callie stopped and turned on him.

"Cameron, go in the house and find Mardi. The two of you need a bath."

"But mom."

"Go!" She hated snapping at him, but if Jason was going to threaten her, it would not be in front of her son.

"Ah, so now I have your attention, do I?" Jason said with a smirk.

CHAPTER FIVE

Patric stood behind the trellis and listened to the exchange. He didn't want to eavesdrop, but if he moved they'd know he'd heard it all. Why would she even listen to this jerk? From the timbre of his voice, he was a pretty good sized guy, and Callie definitely held a fear of him. Whether it were from fear or anger, her voice shook with every word she said.

"What exactly do you want, Jason? I know it can't have anything to do with Cameron."

"Oh, but you are wrong. As usual. It has everything to do with him. I'm sure you know I've remarried."

She felt no jealousy, only pity for the new bride. "What does this have to do with us?"

"Well, since it's just you and me, my new wife and her parents are real big on family. I really don't want a whining baby around all the time, so I think Cameron would make Isabel very happy."

"You insensitive—" Out of anger her hand shot up to slap him, but he caught her by the wrist.

"Ouch," she whimpered.

"Don't you ever raise your hand to me again. You have that child because I was man enough to make him, and no other reason. You have had the precious little thing to yourself for eight years. Now it's my turn."

"You can't have my son. I don't care if your wife is the Queen of Sheba. You'll never use him the way you used me."

"Oh, Callie, you give yourself too much credit. I never used you. You had nothing to offer. Absolutely nothing. And looking at this place, and the way you're raising my son, it doesn't seem to be any different now."

"*I hate you.*"

Patric heard the tears in her voice and wanted to go to her. He'd heard the same pain so many times in his mother's voice.

"I don't care how you feel about me. You work out a visiting schedule, or the lawyers will."

"Get the hell out of here."

"For now, Callie, but I'll be back. Trust me."

Patric waited until the tires on the gravel could no longer be heard, before making his way to the front stairs. He'd panicked at first when Cameron had run off and left him standing, but had soon realized he was up against the house. He felt along the wood until he reached the porch railing. He stopped when he heard the sniffling. For a second or two, he thought it was Cameron, but then something inside him told him who it was. "Callie, is that you?"

"Oh, you scared me. I didn't see you there." He heard her take a soft breath and try to steady her voice.

"Now there's irony for ya." He waited for a laugh, but didn't truly expect one. "Are you okay?"

"Nothing I can't handle. But thanks." Her footsteps moved away from him and panic worked him over again.

"Uh, Callie. Do you think maybe you could wait a minute?"

As much as he hated it, he knew he needed help finding his way back into the house. Something about uncharted territory made him nervous. "I could use a little bit of navigational assistance." He tried to sound as macho as he could.

"Oh my goodness. What are you doing out here? They said you hadn't been outside in—well, a long time."

"I thought I might plow the fields, but it seems as though someone moved my fields." He forced a chuckle and moved to lean nonchalantly against the railing. Only the railing wasn't where he remembered it to be.

Callie caught his arm as his shoulder slipped between the two posts. Thank goodness he couldn't see her grin. The almighty Mr. I—don't—need—anyone, was in desperate need.

"I didn't know you were out here." She stopped. He must have heard Jason and her arguing. "I'm sorry about my ex-husband. I don't know how he found me here, but I promise I won't let him bother you again."

"What is it with you anyway?"

"What? I don't know what you mean." And that was the truth.

"The man comes back into your life after what I can only assume was an unpleasant divorce, tells you he's going to use your kid, and you tell me you're sorry?"

She decided not to say anything about the fact that he had obviously been listening to every word that had been said. After all, she was living in his house. "I know this is my job, and he has caused trouble here for you, so if you have to let me go, I will understand."

"Holy hell, woman!" he shouted. "The man is obviously the scum of the earth and you let him walk all over you."

"I don't see how my relationship with him is any—"

"When he stepped foot on my property, he made it my business." Patric took a deep breath and steadied his nerves. It all rang too familiar for him. "Don't let him have his way."

"It's not that simple. You don't know the whole story."

"Good Lord, what's to know? If you loved each other you'd still be married. If he loved Cameron, he'd have come calling a long time ago."

"How do you expect me to fight him? He's got too much money and too many powerful friends."

"I've got money. If you want to fight him, you can take what you need."

Callie wasn't sure who was more shocked by his proposal, but in a pinch, she'd pick him. "You don't mean that."

"Don't tell me what I mean, damn it. I have so much money I could spit quarters for weeks and never put a dent in it. What the hell good does it do a monster like me?"

Anger rolled around him in waves and surrounded them both. Worse than that was the pain she saw when he referred to himself.

"Who the hell am I going to spend my vast fortune on?" He tipped his head back and sighed. "I gave up on miracles a long time ago. If my money can't do me any good, it should be able to help someone else."

She couldn't imagine what he was feeling. She wanted to reach out and tell him he wasn't a monster. She could see the good in him; why couldn't he see it in himself? He didn't need eyes for that. "Thank you, but I can't."

"What, my money isn't good enough for you? You'd rather let that bastard take your son away?" He took a hesitant step forward. "Fine, whatever."

"It's not that."

"Forget I offered. I would like you to take me to my room."

"But, Patric—"

"Now!"

"You of all people should understand about pride." She spoke softly, so he couldn't hear the tears in her voice.

"You and I are two different people. You don't know anything about me."

"But I do. I know that you hate yourself for whatever reason, and that makes you angry. So very angry."

"You think you are so smart. Well, if that's the case, why are you letting this jerk take your son away?"

The dam broke and she couldn't stop the flow of tears. Torrents of anger, and denial, and fear washed over her, drowning her in a multitude of emotions. "I don't know what to do," she sobbed. "How can I fight the court system? Or my husband? You don't know what he is like. Clever, manipulative...."

"Callie, stop crying."

He reached for her and caught her by the hand. She let him pull her into his arms. Before she could stop it from happening her legs gave out and they both fell to the ground. She landed partly in Patric's lap and clung to him with every ounce of energy she had left. "You don't understand what it's like to be this afraid."

"I don't? How can you say that?"

Patric rocked her back and forth as he talked softly to her. "The day I woke up in the hospital and they told me I'd never see again, I knew my life was over. It was just a matter of time before the rest of my worthless body died."

"Don't say that."

Callie looked up at him. His gaze was pointed off

toward the sky.

"Face it. I'm no good to anyone, including myself. For as far back as I can remember, my father made sure I knew my value. Zero. Jason has done that to you. Is that what you want for your son?"

"No, I don't. But I know Jason."

She snuggled into his arms more closely. "Jason is wrong about Cameron, and me. Just like your father was wrong about you." Callie relaxed in his arms and let the warmth of his body seep into her own. Everything about him felt different. The cold man she'd been avoiding had a heart, and she could feel it beating against her chest. How could she ever make him believe how much she needed him? "You aren't worthless. I need you, and Cameron needs you."

His next words were uttered in a tone so flat and cold that she felt as though she had been doused with ice water. "I authorize your pay-check every week. That's all I've been to anyone for a very long time. I know it, and you know it. So, let's just figure out what you're going to do and work from there."

Angrier than she'd ever been, Callie pulled out of his embrace. "I'm going to take you inside and then I'm going to go and make my son let me hug him. I'll work out my own problems."

"Think about what I said."

"Oh, of that you can be sure. I sure won't forget it, Mr LeClerc." She stood up and helped him to his feet before leading him up the front steps. When they got inside the door, he stepped away from her.

"Thanks for getting me back on familiar ground."

"It's my job. Next time you feel the need to wander off alone, let me know. I'd hate for you to get lost in the woods."

Patric entered the dining room to find his supper already served, Callie gone, and only the scent of rose water lingered behind. He ate his meal in silence, using the time to contemplate the events of the day. In a matter of a few short days, his quiet existence had become chaotic. The memories of the life he'd once known had been reborn. Blindness was all he'd been able to depend on since the accident. Now he found himself wanting to depend on Callie, but he couldn't. How could he ask of her what he couldn't offer himself?

"I can't find my mom."

Patric jumped at the sound of Cameron's voice. Damn, he couldn't even hear a clomping child.

"I don't know where she is. I'm sure she's fine."

"I don't think so. He makes her cry. Like you did."

Cameron's words slammed into his chest like a lead ball. Cameron had to be wrong. He'd done nothing to make his employee cry. Anything he'd asked he'd had a right—what right? He'd yelled, he'd insulted, he'd been a class-act jerk. "Cameron, when did I make your mother cry?"

"A few days ago, when you told us we had to leave. She was sad because we didn't have any place to be our home. I think she likes it here."

"Why don't you live with your dad any more?"

Rights. He had no right to pry into their lives. Callie had made it more than clear that his help wasn't welcome.

"He was mean and he hurt my mom all the time."

Patric sat up straight in his chair. He heard Cameron scuffing his toe on the carpeted floor and felt his nervousness. "You don't have to tell me if you don't want."

"He hit mom and he said mean things to her. He said mom was ugly and that's not true."

"I'm sure you're right. Tell me about your mom. What does she look like?" Patric opened his mind and let it go blank, he pushed aside all the preconceived images he'd made of Callie.

"Her hair is pretty brown. It makes me think of the syrup she puts on my pancakes."

Patric remembered the image of breakfast on the patio with his mother. The creamy shine that covered his waffles. He imagined what it would look like with the sun warming the strands against her skin.

"She has skin like creamy coffee, and pretty green eyes, dark like Rupert's."

"Who's Rupert?"

Cameron laughed. "Rupert was the toad I had when we first left for our own house. He was green and sparkled when he got wet."

Emeralds. Patric remembered the emerald ring his mother had received at Christmas, the last Christmas before he had gone off to school. The flecks of the sparkling stone had mesmerized him as a child, and the idea of Callie's eyes opened a door in him he'd worked hard to keep locked. The crying he'd heard earlier had wrenched his heart and he knew, he envisioned what they would look like, if he could only see them.

"Why do you look funny? Am I saying something wrong?" Cameron reached out and took his hand, something few people had ever done.

"No, I'm just a little tired. Our little trip took a lot out of me."

"You're not gonna tell mom, are you? I mean, I'm

not s'posed to be bothering you and she'd be mad at me."

"I think we'll keep this our little secret. The same as our little talk tonight. Okay?" Patric shook the boy's hand and they agreed. Cameron was his first friend in years and quite honestly, he liked it. All he had to do now was figure out how to make Callie let him help. Then he had to figure out how he could help.

"I'm gonna go look in the kitchen again. I'll see you tomorrow."

"Good night, kid."

The throbbing in Patric's head grew with each passing moment and he felt the familiar nausea in his stomach. The doctor's words rang out in his head like a booming drum, "You can't get upset, or it will put pressure on the nerves. You have to stay calm."

How could he stay calm in this damn helpless state? How many more people could he let down before God put him out of his misery? He stumbled up from the table and counted his steps toward the staircase. Why didn't he have his damn pills in his pocket? He had always had them in his pocket, until Callie had come along. He hadn't taken one of the tiny tablets in over a week.

"God, not now."

He made it up to his room with only a few new bruises and one hell of a bad attitude. He popped the pill into his mouth and fell into bed, fully clothed.

He pressed his fingertips against his temples and rubbed gently. Gradually, the pressure decreased and he was able to open his eyes against the tightness. Breathtaking. Her hair glowed under the pale moonlight, and her eyes gazed directly into his. And he saw them. His heart raced with the excitement of sight.

He reached up and stroked the golden brown curls.

Her exquisitely heart shaped face held the radiance of an angel, bright and seductive. He brushed his thumb across her cheek and marveled at how the blush swept over it so sweetly. Pale crimson blended with the creamy tones of her flesh. The moon caught flecks of lightness in her green eyes and he stared. Unable to look away, he leaned closer. She lowered her lashes before sighing. How much could one person take before they dissolved into ecstasy? His entire body reacted to the feel of her hand on his chest. Every muscle in his body tightened with a desire unlike he'd ever known. Her fingertip pressed against his bare flesh and left a trail of heat down to the top of his pants, exquisite, painfully torturous heat.

When her lips touched his, reality exploded into shards of brilliant light. Patric closed his eyes against the brightness, then forced them back open. He opened his mouth and tasted her sweetness. Her tongue licked hesitantly at his.

A moment later, he pulled her tighter against him. Their mouths became one and their bodies melted together into a perfect form. Her hands moved from one part of his body to the next, touching, tormenting, and igniting new levels of passion.

Something in the back of Patric's mind nudged him and he drifted back into darkness. A small noise pulled him from his dream and doused him with the wave of reality. The sound reached him again and he pushed back the sweat-drenched sheet and sat up. His feet hit the cold wood floor and he came fully awake. A second later the condition of his body distracted him from the sound. The tightness in his stomach reached the lower regions of his body and a groan echoed across his room. "This can't be happening to me."

A sob reached his ears and the sound of its sadness wrapped around his heart and squeezed. He knew immediately that it was Callie crying. He had to go to her. Lord help him, he shouldn't, but he had to. He pushed himself up off the bed and counted himself to the door. He took his time getting to the staircase landing. He paused and listened for Callie's sobs.

His chest grew tighter with each step he took toward her. By the time he knocked on her bedroom door he could barely breathe. "Callie, can I come in?"

The crying stopped and he heard her shuffling around the room. "Just a minute. Let me straighten up a bit." Her voice shook with each word, and he wanted to be the one to make it steady again.

"Come on, Callie, I'm blind for Christ's sake. I can't see." He silently cursed the harshness of his tone. "It doesn't matter. Can I come in?"

He heard the door click and felt the breeze from the overhead fan in her room. His hair, clean for a change, caught and blew back from his forehead. His body still damp from the impact of his dream, cooled with the air. He suddenly remembered he wasn't wearing a shirt. He considered going back to his room and getting a shirt, but wondered what it would matter. It wasn't like he had anything she'd be interested in.

Callie stood inside the room. The heat from the hallway wrapped around her as she stared at the sight before her. Patric's chest heaved from his labored breathing. It was perfectly sculpted chest, not as pale as the last time she'd seen it, with a layer of chestnut hair. The hairline stopped abruptly just above his stomach and faded into a line of scarred flesh. Her eyes rested only briefly on the scars before roving lower toward the waistband of his jeans.

"I heard you crying and came to make sure everything is okay." Patric reached over for the doorframe and then leaned against it.

Everything about him screamed of virility. The tousled state of his his long wavy hair, the glisten of sweat on his skin, and the way his body took up nearly every inch of space in her range of vision. The crooked tilt of his lips gave him a slightly wicked look, framed as they were by the beard he had taken great pains to trim neatly. All of this was combined with startling gray eyes, which could scare off even the bravest of souls. But Callie wasn't scared. She was intrigued. Staring at him, for a brief moment, she forgot her troubles and something else gnawed at her insides. Something she knew she should ignore.

"Thank you, I—I'm fine."

"That's why I heard your bawling across the house?" He stood tall and turned to walk away.

She didn't want him to go. She didn't necessarily want him to stay, but having him near seemed to help her forget. "I didn't mean to be so loud, I just—"

"Look, you don't need to explain anything to me. I just didn't want you waking up the kid. He hates it when you cry."

Callie looked at him, glad he couldn't see her surprised expression. "How do you know that?"

After several false starts he finally gave up. "Well, hell, every kid hates to see his mother cry." A shadow of something painful crossed over his expression before it turned hard again. "How else would I know?"

"I don't know. I just thought maybe—oh, never mind. I'm sorry I woke you up." Callie turned away from Patric, embarrassment burning in her cheeks. Jason had always hated it when she cried, which had happened quite frequently while they had been married.

"Callie, I know it's none of my business, but if you have a problem, I might be able to help. I mean I know I'm limited, but at least I could listen. It's one of the few things I can still do." Disgust, more than likely with himself, tinged his voice.

"It's not anything anyone can help me with. Jason has too many people in his corner and there's nothing I can do to fight him."

The tears started again and before she could stop them, she was, as Patric had put it, bawling. She covered her eyes with her hands and cried, unaware that Patric had moved until he bumped into her. His arms came up and she fell into his embrace.

With each sob his hold on her tightened until she had to pull away. "Patric—"

"Sorry, I didn't mean to do that. I know you probably don't want someone like me touching you." He slowly backed away from her, toward the door.

"What are you talking about?"

"I don't know what made me think you'd give a damn if I listened to you or not. Since you're okay, I'll go back to my room." His back bumped the doorframe and he swore.

"Patric, wait."

"No, I was out of line."

"Patric, I liked it." Her words stopped him before he could make it out of the room. "It's the first time anyone has ever done that."

"What, held you? Obviously not if you have a son."

Callie smiled, but it didn't erase the sadness. "Sex

doesn't always constitute love, or even caring." She considered all the times she'd told Jason no, and he'd exercised his husbandly rights anyway. Their sexual relationship had never been mutual. She'd loved him once, before the first slap, and even for a time after the tenth.

His hands clenched by his sides and the muscles in his shoulders and neck visibly tightened. "Your husband raped you?"

"No court of law would see it that way. I never fought him, and he was my husband."

"And that makes it right? That's not how it was taught to me." He turned and stepped back into the room.

"Why don't you come and sit down. You're making me nervous standing there."

"Are you sure? I don't want to make you uncomfortable."

"It's ok so long as we keep our voice down. Cameron is sleeping next door. It was good of you to let him have a room of his own. Thank you."

"You cleaned it up. It was the least I could do."

"Thanks all the same. And for coming to see if I was all right. Come in a sit a minute."

She walked over and took his hand. At first he pulled against her, then relaxed and followed her to the bed. It didn't occur to her at first to be nervous, but as the mattress gave under their weight she looked at him. He faced her, but stared past her. Something in the way his jaw set told her he wasn't as sure about the situation.

"Aren't you afraid I might take advantage of you?" He spoke softly, sounding almost vulnerable.

"Patric, if I felt threatened by you, I would have locked my door when you knocked. You might scare everyone else, but I've been through too much to worry about it. Besides, if you try anything, I'll just run."

"I can run too, you know."

"Yeah, but only until you hit the first wall."

Deep laughter rolled out of him. Callie smiled.

"Good point." He stopped laughing and let his head hang back. "I can't remember the last time I laughed. I can't remember the last time anyone wasn't afraid of me."

"It's not so bad. Is it?" Callie reached out and brushed a few stray hairs back away from his forehead. His hand reached up and caught hers. He grasped her gently and his hand trembled as he held hers. "Patric?"

He tried to let go, but she held on tighter. "You don't have to—"

"I know I don't, but I want to."

"I started to tell you before, that no one has ever held me like that before. I mean, because they cared. People don't usually worry about me, only Cameron."

"He's a good kid. He loves you a lot." He stopped. "You seem to know an awful lot about how my son feels. Would you care to tell me how you know?"

"No."

"Don't mess with him. He is all I have in this world and if you do anything to hurt him, I swear I'll make you pay." Her body went rigid with fierce protectiveness.

"Why don't you save that attitude for that ass you were married to. Seems to me you're gonna need it to fight him."

The tears started again. "I told you, I can't fight him. He's a lawyer and he has money." She leaned against him when he wrapped an arm around her. "I can barely survive, much less hire an attorney to fight a custody battle."

"Callie, I may be blind, but I can still see some things.

I see how much your son means to you and I see how much you mean to him. I heard what your ex said and it makes me sick to think you would let him do something so vile."

His hand stroked her cheek as she cried against his chest. "It's not that. I just don't have the means."

"But I do."

CHAPTER SIX

She raised her head and looked at him. "I thought I already told you--"

His mouth lowered slowly until their lips met. His thumb traced along her lower lip as he kissed her. Nothing made sense, not his concern, or the kiss. A kiss like none she'd ever known. When he finally moved back, she could only stare at him.

"Well, I know one way to get you to stop talking." His already wicked grin spread across his face. His hand remained on her face and she soaked in all of its warmth and offer of assurance.

"Was that all you were doing? Making me shut up?" It bothered her that he might not have been affected by her as she was by him. In truth, the kiss had opened a door she'd worked hard to keep sealed. The longer he stroked her skin, the more confused she grew. The man had little to no feelings for anyone, including himself, and yet he'd managed to make her feel for him.

"Callie, I don't exactly know what I'm doing. I only know that I can't make myself stop. But I have to." He stood up and carefully made his way to the door. "I can help you keep Cameron if it's what you really want, and I know it is." He left without another word.

Callie fell back on the bed and fought for air. The scent of his masculinity lingered around her. She reached up and let her own fingertips brush against the cheek he'd held so tenderly. A chill raced through her and she considered the kiss. Sweet lips, chapped, but not rough. She touched her lips and sighed. The breath on her hand reminded her of his breath just before their lips met. What was she thinking? He was her patient, and her behavior had got her the best job she'd ever had. No, she couldn't get involved with Patric LeClerc, no matter how sexy he looked standing next to her bed without a shirt. She sat straight up. "I didn't hear you come back in."

"I didn't want to just walk away. This is the first time in years I've wanted something enough to admit it."

She swallowed and took a deep breath. "What exactly do you want?"

"I'm not sure, but I know it involves you." He turned and walked back out.

Callie waited a few minutes before deciding to follow. When she stepped out of the hall, she expected to see him nearing the steps, but he she didn't see him, and she didn't hear him. She ran down the steps and up into the other wing. She knocked lightly on his door, but there was no answer. Having no idea where he could have gone, she decided to go down to the library and find a book to read.

Patric stood completely still inside the study door and listened to Callie as she passed by. For a moment, he feared she might come into the study, but she moved on to the next room. He waited until he heard her feet treading back up the stairs before going to sit down.

He rested his head on the cushioned chair and tried to catch his breath. Had he really told her he wanted her? What kind of fool would do a stupid thing like that? His heart racing in his chest branded him a class A fool. Oh well, the damage had been done. Now he would have to figure what he meant and what he could do about it. He closed his eyes trying to gather his thoughts.

He woke up suddenly when the warmth of the sun hit his face. "There better be a damn good reason you keep opening the drapes."

"Well, it does make it easier to see where I'm going if I have a little bit of light. And good morning to you too, sunshine."

"Cute. Is breakfast ready?" Patric smelled the bacon and knew it was. She'd made a point of feeding him up every morning. And he'd put on a few pounds because of it.

"Cameron and I are going on a picnic this afternoon. He seems to be under the impression you might want to go."

"Hmm."

Patric held out his hand and warmed when Callie took it. Together they walked to the dining room. He stopped her when she started to leave. "Where are you going?"

"I'm going to go feed my son. I do that sometimes. Besides, your breakfast is getting cold. Go and eat."

A memory from the past flashed in Patric's mind and he saw his parents sitting at the table with him. Letty served breakfast while his father read the newspaper, ignoring him, and his mother chatted about the day's upcoming events. A hollow spot opened inside him, like something was missing.

"I'll come clear the dishes when you're finished."

The sound of Callie's voice was the answer. Every day he sat at a huge table and ate his meals, alone. "Wouldn't it be easier if the two of you ate in here with me? I mean at least that way you would only have to clean up one room."

"If you're sure you don't mind. The kitchen does get kinda stuffy."

Callie called Cameron, who bolted into the dining room at a dead run.

"What, mom?" He skidded to a halt and bumped into the back of Patric's chair. "Oh, sorry, sir. I didn't mean to--"

Patric smiled. He always knew when Cameron was around. It hadn't taken him long to get used to the child at all. He actually enjoyed the kid's enthusism.

"Your mom says you two are going on a picnic today. Where ya taking her?"

"I thought I'd go to the same place we—I mean I went the other day. She said maybe you might like to go with us."

"Really? And here I was under the impression it was you who might enjoy my company."

So it was Callie who wanted to spend time with him. Lord knows why, but thank goodness. Since his outing with Cameron he'd wanted to go back into the sunlight. He wanted to feel the grass against the bottom of his feet, and he wanted to relax. He'd lived for too long with his own self-imposed imprisonment. Was it possible he could have a real life with someone who didn't care if he was blind or not? Did it really not matter to Callie? Hope soared through him.

"So, are you going to join us or not?"

"If you eat meals with me, I'll picnic with you."

"Deal."

Cameron bounced around the room, squealing with delight. "Yeah!"

Breakfast was a buzz of conversation, mostly

Cameron's. He chattered on about the toad he'd seen on the patio. He told them, in great detail, about the nest of worms he'd managed to uncover under the porch of the house. Patric laughed at the sound of Callie squirming in her chair. Mealtime as a child had never been this way for him. His father had paid little attention to him and his mother, and when he did it had only been to tell them to shut up.

Callie cleared away the last of the dirty dishes from the table while Cameron talked Patric into a stupor. "So when are we going?"

Patric sighed. "Well, maybe we could let your mother finish doing the breakfast dishes."

"We could go without her, and she could catch up after she fixes our lunch."

Callie spun around and stared him down. "Cameron, you'll do no such thing."

He blushed under her maternal glare. "Sorry."

"Maybe you should go get your room cleaned up."

"Why do I have to clean my room and he—" Cameron clamped his hand over his mouth. "Never mind, I'll go clean." He looked toward Patric before leaving the room.

"Do you have any idea what my son is talking about?" She directed her question at Patric who sat with his hands folded in front of him with his face raised toward the ceiling. "Patric?"

"Oh, what?" he asked innocently.

"I asked you a question. Do you have any idea what Cameron's big secret is?"

"What makes you think he has one?" He paused. "I mean, don't kids say strange things?" He clicked his fingertips on the hardwood table. A nervous gesture?

"I suppose. I just get the feeling there is something I

should be seeing here." Callie stepped toward the door.

"Yeah, me too." The sad tone of his voice stopped her.

"Patric—" She started to apologize for her insensitivity, but he stopped her. They'd come a long way in a short time. A week earlier she would have been packing her bags, unemployed.

Now, he teased her, and made her son laugh.

"If you don't get a move on, your son is going to burst at the seams."

Patric stood and pushed his chair against the table. "I've got something to do before we head out. Buzz, when you're ready."

Twenty minutes later Callie rolled her aching shoulders. The tension seeped into her spirits, and Jason's face popped into her mind. She still had no idea how she would keep him from taking Cameron away. For hours, she'd lain in bed thinking of the right words to use in her explanation to Cameron. How could you tell a child they were going to have to spend time with someone they barely knew, much less liked? Her heart ached inside her chest and she leaned over the sink. A tear slipped down her cheek, but she brushed it away with an angry swipe. *No, you won't ruin this for us. I won't let you.* She pushed Jason's image away and went to work packing lunch.

After setting the basket by the kitchen door, she went in search of the boys. She found Cameron digging around in a downstairs fireplace and sent him out into the yard to wait for her. She had to search four rooms before she located Patric. Metal clanged against metal as she reached the work-out room door. Remembering the last time she'd seen him in this room, she cleared her throat and made her presence known. "Cameron is downstairs waiting for us."

Her mouth went dry when he sat up and faced her. She examined the difference in his physical appearance. The skin of his arms and torso glowed with new color. Not a drastic change, but enough to know he'd actually gone outside. Small moisture-filled blisters marred his otherwise smooth shoulders. The waistband of his pants hung low around his hips, exposing a narrow line of paler skin, a sharp contrast to the newly-burned flesh.

"I need to change first." He sat on the weight bench staring in her direction. "Are you sure you don't mind me tagging along?"

"Patric, we both want you to come along. Besides, the sunlight will do you some good. I know you haven't been outside in a while."

Callie backed away from the door when he walked toward her. The scent of his physical exertion wafted around her and her senses whirled. The musky odor mixed with his sweat-slicked body held her captive. Her eyes focused on the thin line of hair in the middle of his chest and without her consent followed the trail down to the top of his sweats. At the end of her journey she found a treasure she hadn't expected and her heart raced. Desire slammed through her, leaving her nearly breathless.

Patric stood still in the doorway facing her. "Is something wrong?"

She looked at his lips, lips so full they begged her to lean forward and kiss them. When they moved his jaw flexed in a most intoxicating way.

"Callie, are you all right?"

The gray flecks in his eyes shone glassy and mesmerized her. The sound of his voice drummed through her like a roll of thunder on a stormy night leaving her wet and quivering. His touch—

"Callie, what is it?"

His hand shook her gently and she realized he'd been talking to her. "I'm sorry, I'm fine."

"You didn't answer me." His fingers brushed against the back of her hand and her skin sizzled, soft against his hard finger tips. Her hand trembled in his. She couldn't be afraid of him. He'd made a point of not yelling and he hadn't fired her in days. Hell, he hadn't even barked in his blasted intercom. Her breath blew across his cheek in short gasps. Maybe she wasn't feeling well. He reached up for her cheek, but he only made it as far as her neck. A soft sigh reached his ears and she tensed under his touch. He pulled away, but she held his hand.

"Don't stop."

He barely heard her request, but the implications shot through him in record time. Callie wasn't sick and she wasn't tired. He let her pull his hand back up to her cheek and she leaned into it. His thumb brushed along the softness of her eyelashes. Her eyes closed. "Callie?"

"Patric." She turned her lips into his palm and his body took the brunt of the shock wave. The sound of her voice melted his self-control and he leaned closer. "Is this what you want?" he asked around the lump in his throat.

Their lips met and everything changed. Sweet ecstasy worked a hazy web around them as her tongue danced against his. Each thrust pulled him deeper into the mist of pleasure until he spiraled downward. He reached out to steady himself. His arms pressed around her and he pulled her closer. Her breasts pushed against him as she arched her back.

Second by second, the kiss deepened until his entire body responded with its own actions. He stepped forward until he had Callie pressed against the far wall. He pulled his hands from behind her and searched out the soft curves of her breasts. As he cupped her gently, she thrust her hands in his hair and a moan slipped out. Her response to their kiss undid him and he ground against her. "Callie, it's been—"

"Too long," she finished. Then she fused her mouth against his.

Suddenly she pushed against him. "What's wrong? Did I do something wrong?" He stepped back too quickly and stumbled over his own foot. He reached out for the wall, but found her hand instead.

"Patric, it's okay. It's not you."

He moved forward as he spoke. "Then why did you stop?" He kissed her once, then again.

"Mmm. Cameron is waiting downstairs." She took his lip between her teeth and sighed. "Maybe we can finish this later."

Patric took a deep breath and raked his fingers through his hair. "We'd better get downstairs." He put his hand against the wall and walked toward the stairs.

Callie watched him as his hand slid along the hallway wall and he counted his steps. Would he ever regain his sight? Modern technology had to have an operation for something like this. She'd call the office later and see if anyone had any ideas or knew of any specialists.

She followed Patric downstairs and into the kitchen where they found Cameron waiting.

"I smell vanilla."

Callie laughed. "That's because my son has helped himself to a bowl of ice cream." She crossed her arms over her chest and leaned against the wall. "When you're finished, we can go on our outing."

An hour later they found the spot Cameron had raved about to Patric. Callie led them all to a small clearing and decided they would stop there. Patric held out his hand and felt for anything close to him. His hand brushed against a tree and he stepped closer and let his back rest on the moist bark. He waited for one of the others to lead him to the blanket. The blanket swished through the air and settled with a slight rustle on the leaf-covered ground. Still Patric waited.

"Two steps straight forward." Callie's soft voice melted into his mind and exploded into his senses.

He stepped forward and knelt down. His knees landed on the blanket. For the first time, he experienced something close to independence. Cameron's small hand picked his up and wrapped it around a cold soda can. He moved his thumb across the top, feeling for an opening. He tilted the can up and took a drink. He missed covering part of the opening and a stream of soda dripped down his chin. Before he could reach up, Callie's fingertips caught the soda and wiped it away. His breath caught and his heart pounded in his chest. Her rosewater scent lingered and wreaked havoc with his senses.

"Do you want a glass?"

Patric shook his head. If they could drink from the can, he could too. He sat and listened while Callie laid the food out onto the blanket. Cameron squirmed and wiggled until Callie gave him her approval to investigate their surroundings. After the boy had run off, the climate changed considerably. Callie moved to his side of the blanket and took his hand in hers.

"Patric, we need to talk."

"About what?" He moved his thumb back and forth across the top of her hand. He could hardly believe his own actions. With little experience with women and most of it bad, he wanted to do this right. "Is something wrong?

"I don't think so. Actually, I'm afraid it's too right. I took this job because I need the money and I need a place for my son and me to live."

Patric pulled his hand away. Pain ricocheted through his entire body before slamming into his heart. Damn fool! He should have known better. "Well, I'm glad my estate and I could be of service to you." He made no effort to disguise his sarcasm.

"Patric, that's not what I meant." She reached for his hands, but he pulled away from her touch. "Please."

"No, you've made your needs perfectly clear and I think we would do good to remember them."

He turned himself away from the sound of her breathing. Her hands rested on his shoulders and she pulled him back around to face her. He tried to lean away, but she didn't allow it.

"Damn you, Patric. Listen to me. I'm trying to tell you something. I'm not sure I can work for you any longer."

Patric's heart lurched into his throat and cold fear gripped his insides, but pride stepped in before he could stop it. "I see. Are you giving me notice, again?"

Callie sighed. "No, you don't see. I think I'm in—"

Cameron's footsteps rushed through the leaves and he skidded to a halt next to them. "Mom, let's go swimming."

"Cameron, Patric and I are in the middle of something."

"No, little man. I think that's a good idea." He pulled away from her and held out his hand. "Give me a hand up and we'll make some waves."

Callie watched her chance walk away into the forest. "You already have." She'd almost told him she thought she might be in love with him. Thank God Cameron had come along or she might have ruined everything. His reaction told her all she needed to know. She wasn't sure of her feelings, and he didn't want her love.

They ate lunch in strained silence, both listening to Cameron chatter on about all the things he'd seen in the woods. The afternoon passed quickly, and they began their walk back as the sun lowered in the sky. Callie watched the colors melt into an array of pinks and oranges, then begin to fade into darkness. She walked around the corner of the house and saw the headlights coming up the gravel drive. She recognized the car and her heart stopped.

"Who is it, Callie?" Patric asked.

"I'll take care of it. Would you please take Cameron in and get him settled in his room. I'll be right in."

"Mom, don't talk to him."

"*Go*, Cameron. I'll be in soon."

She hated being short with him, but she couldn't risk him overhearing anything until she'd resolved the problem.

Jason stepped out of the car and walked toward her. She'd never noticed his cocky swagger before. Tension crackled between them. She followed his eyes in the direction of Patric and Cameron, carrying their picnic gear into the front door.

CHAPTER SEVEN

"Well, Callie, a little family outing with the invalid?"

Jason's callous tone and disregard for Patric's feelings made her skin crawl, and her palm itched to slap the smug expression off his face. His arrogance grated on her last nerve and she took a step forward. A combination of her anger at Patric's unyielding attitude and Jason's crappy one gave her a shot of inner strength, but Jason killed it quickly.

"Callie, I have a present for you." He turned and signaled the man in the car to join them. The suited man came forward and handed her a box. The silver foil wrapping chilled her to the touch.

"I don't want it." She pushed it back into the man's hands. Jason snatched it away and shoved it into hers.

"Take the damn box and open it," he snarled.

"I don't know what kind of game you're playing, but I don't want to be involved." Callie held the package, but didn't open it.

He stepped up to her and lowered his face close enough to hers for her to feel his breath and smell the liquor. "You became involved when you spread your skinny little legs to a man far out of your league." His fingers dug into her arm.

"Jason, stop it. It's finished." She pulled against his grip, but he didn't let go until the other man touched his shoulder.

"Callie, open the box. Now!"

Her hands trembled as she took the lid off. She looked up at him, confused when she saw the contents. "What are you doing, Jason?" Her voice shook and she struggled for control.

"Listen to me and listen good. I will have visitation with my son, and it will be at my discretion. If you fight me, I will take him from you and the only thing you'll have left is that picture from his birth." He pressed his mouth against hers and thrust his tongue deep inside.

She shoved him away hard. Callie choked down the bile rising in her throat. "You're sick."

"You think?" He threw his head back and laughed. "Then you won't be surprised to look under that picture and find the papers announcing my suit for custody of Cameron." He laughed again. "You gotta love me."

He waved at her, smirking, and got back into the car. He drove off in a cloud of dust which choked her.

Callie stood in the front yard for an eternity before she stumbled blindly into the house. She barely remembered making Patric and Cameron dinner, or going out into the side yard.

Cameron came out once, but she sent him to bed with a mechanical kiss and a hug she barely felt. No tears came, only disgust and fear. Too angry to cry and too scared to think, s sat outside and stared up at Cameron's bedroom window until she saw the light go out. Then she stood to go inside.

She saw a shadow on the porch then.

"He's worried about you. He thinks he's done something wrong."

"I'll take care of my son. Don't worry about it."

Callie walked past Patric and left him standing on

the side porch. She all but ran up to Cameron's room. She stopped outside the door and listened for sounds. When his soft snore reached her ears, she turned the knob and went in. His small body lay curled up in the center of the bed, surrounded by an array of action figures and mechanical objects. She pushed some out of the way and lay down next to him.

His breathing changed and he rolled onto his side, putting his back to her. She moved to spoon herself around him and lay with him until his breathing evened out again. At some point during the night ,she got up and stumbled to her own room.

Callie fell across her bed. How could Jason do this to her? He truly planned to take Cameron away. Before she could stop them, tears rolled down her cheeks, leaving a burning trail of disgust and pain. Her shoulders shook as sobs wracked her body. How much more hurt could Jason pile on top of her?

"Callie? Are you all right?" She started at the sound of Patric's voice.

"Go away."

"I can't. And I don't think you really want to be alone anyway." He moved into the room and stepped carefully toward the bed. "What's this all about?"

"It doesn't matter. There's nothing I can do."

She fell back onto the bed and resumed her crying. Patric reached out to her. His hand settled on her leg. She looked up at him, amazed to see tears in his eyes. "I can't fight anymore."

"I can't either."

She sat up and stared into his handsome face. The pale scars of his accident called out to be healed from the inside. She wanted to reach out and stroke each deviation from perfection. An image of her tongue tracing the jagged line from the corner of his eye down to his cheek turned her thoughts in a new direction. His words threatened to pull her back.

"You don't have to fight me now. Why don't you just let go?"

"It hurts."

"I know," he choked out. He lowered his head and his arms hung to his sides.

As much pain showed in his face as beat in her heart. Only it wasn't her pain. He had his own demons to fight, and the thought of him suffering brought her up short. She touched his hand and breathed a sigh when he held hers. The contact of flesh against flesh pushed aside all thoughts of Jason. Patric pulled her up off the bed and she leaned into his embrace. His arms offered the safety and warmth she needed to take the edge off her nervousness, and she relaxed.

"I don't want you to hurt. The thought of someone doing this to you makes me sick," Patric whispered as he stroked her hair.

Gently, his fingers twisted around the soft curls framing her face. His fingertip brushed against her cheek and she trembled. The scent of the man holding her swirled around, surrounding her in a wave of something instinctive. She titled her head up until her forehead rested against his chin. His hand cupped her cheek a second before his lips touched her skin. She knew she should stop him, but she wanted it to happen. She wanted to taste the saltiness of his skin. She wanted his lips pressed against hers, and more than that, she wanted him to hold her.

"I can help you." Patric's breath blew softly across

her face and nearly undid her.

"I don't know what to do." She meant it. She wanted so much from him, but had no idea how to tell him. Jason took what he wanted and left no choices. She didn't know how to be like him, and didn't want to.

"What do you want to do, Callie?" His voice shook.

"I want—I want to feel something other than pain."

His lips covered hers and it started. He'd given no warning and she silently thanked him as all but her passion for him was swept aside. Heat swept through her as their tongues danced together and his hand brushed up and braced her head from behind. The sensuality of his touch drew her in closer. Everything about him drew her in, his smell, his taste, and his touch. Seconds ticked by before she found the nerve to react from within. She turned full against him and pulled him closer. Their bodies joined into one mass of frenzied movement. Her hands slipped around his neck and she sighed into the kiss.

He slipped his hand down the length of her neck and onto her shoulder, where he worked his fingers under her blouse and she sighed against him. She arched her back against his hand as he moved it toward her breast. Quick breaths intensified their kiss. He wanted her. She wanted him. Something inside her changed, and all of her inhibitions disappeared. "Ooh."

"Do you want me to stop?" he asked against her mouth. "Just tell me."

She closed the short distance he'd made between them and thrust her tongue against his. Her heart raced when he touched her again. Hi shard fingers brushed against the fabric covering her erect nipple and she cried out. It was so good, the feelings grew with each second they stood touching. She took a deep breath and his musky scent worked like an aphrodisiac. Callie moved her hand into his hair and managed to get him closer, as if she would pull all of him into herself.

Soft tendrils of his ebony hair curled around her fingers and she stroked them, mesmerized at their softness. He sighed against her mouth before breaking their kiss. He didn't move away. Instead he lowered his head and pressed his lips to the pulse in her throat. His tongue darted across her earlobe, sending a tremor of feeling through her. Her hands grew adventurous and she pressed them against his chest. A flicker of disappointment touched her when her palms met the cotton of his shirt. Without thought, her fingers moved swiftly to undo the first button, then the next until they reached the waistband of his jeans. She reached behind him and tugged the shirt out of his pants, pushing it down his arms and tossing to the floor.

He sighed and threw his head back when her hands brushed up his back. His cologne wafted around her and she breathed in deeply enjoying the muskiness. Soft tingles raced up and down her body as her hands moved back around to his chest. The soft brush of his hair tickled her palms and she sighed. She lowered her head and brushed her lips against his nipple, eliciting a moan from him. She used her tongue to tempt the small nub into a state of sensitive hardness. With each flick of her tongue he grew more rigid and she grew bolder. At one point she wondered which of their bodies caused the trembling sensation. Perhaps both.

Patric pulled her head back up and covered her mouth again. He trembled from the sensations her tongue caused on his body, but he couldn't bear the loss of her mouth against his. He needed the sweetness and moisture of her tongue thrusting against his. Her hands moved from his shoulder, gently kneading the tension away. A frisson of excitement raced through him and he pulled her roughly against him. All sense of control slipped away and they melded together in perfect unison. His hand slipped between them and he took her breast against his palm. Every image of her beauty he'd ever played out in his mind came into focus with the simple touch.

She arched against him, yet it was he who groaned. He thrust his hips forward and rubbed himself against her, pressing and enjoying the warmth of her body against his. His hand moved up and slipped the fabric of her top down. He circled the small bump on her shoulder before lowering his head down to kiss it. He moved his fingers and his lips lower until she trembled. The curve of her collarbone warmed against his mouth and she titled her head back.

Patric's voice shook when he spoke. "I need to know how beautiful you are." He kissed one spot after another, tasting, discovering, and memorizing. He would never forget the sweetness of her neck, or her mouth. He would never forget the way she moved against him without fear or revulsion.

Callie traced the outline of a scar on his shoulder. The patch of marred skin intrigued and excited her. His body quivered and she leaned in to kiss the spot where her finger had previously been.

"I'm sorry," he whispered.

She stopped and looked up at him. "Why?"

"It must look horrible. I don't usually let people see me without a shirt."

Anger at his words coursed through her and she held

herself still. When she spoke it was slow and deliberate. "You are the most—beautiful man I have ever seen. When I look at you I see something so pure." She kissed his cheek. "You are honest; angry, but honest." She kissed his neck and he sighed. "You take my breath away just walking into a room." She leaned down and took his nipple into her mouth. "See yourself as I do."

"I can't see—"

"As I do." Her hands moved rhythmically with the beating of his heart. Each beat pushed her onward until she touched him from his neck to his waist. She kneeled down in front of him and pushed the button on his jeans through the small hole. Slowly and carefully she lowered the zipper until his dark hair came into view. She pushed his pats down, letting her hands brush against his thighs. Her heart raced when his legs began to tremble.

"No one has ever done that." His raspy voice shook her. Pure emotion, she knew because it was her motivation.

"Perhaps no one has wanted you the way I do." Callie kissed his thigh and he physically shook.

"How can you want me?"

"With everything I have inside me," she whispered. He pulled her up by her arms and their bodies closed together again.

One second slipped into another and time ceased to matter. Everything except his hands touching her ceased to matter.

"Callie, I can't remember the last time I made love to someone."

She kissed him on the mouth. "Good. Then I don't have any competition." Her arms circled around his back and she stepped back toward the bed. He stopped when they bumped the bed.

"I can't."

"Why?" She took his hands in hers.

"I can't see and I'll hurt you. I can't hurt you. I won't hurt you."

At that moment Callie loved him. She fell hopelessly and desperately in love with him. The man in front of her carried years of pain and rejection in his heart and he couldn't hurt her. "Then I won't let you." She turned them so his thighs pressed against the mattress. "Sit."

He lowered himself onto the bed and she pushed him back. He reached up for her, but she pushed his hand away. She purposely dragged her fingernails up the inside of his thighs and reveled in the shudder it evoked. She flicked the inside of his knee with her tongue and he moaned out loud. Higher and higher she kissed until the tip of him brushed against her cheek. She turned her head and carefully took him into her mouth. His entire body shook uncontrollably. She held still until he settled, then began her deliberate assault on his senses.

"Callie—"

"Shh, let me show you how beautiful you are."

Slowly, she stroked him and teased him until her heart raced so fast she feared it might burst. With each stroke of her mouth against his silky flesh, his breathing grew sharper. Her hands caressed the muscles in his thighs as she grew more excited. His fingers dug into the bed sheets next to her head, but he never touched her. She sensed his impending release and reached for it.

"Not like this," he gasped. "I need all of you." He pulled her up onto his body and wrapped his arms around her. For a long time, they lay together, not moving. During that time he never lost his excitement, but his breathing evened out.

Callie raised her head and moved her lips close to his. "Trust me?"

"If I can."

Honesty, a most erotic concept, she thought. "I won't let you hurt me."

"How can I not?" he asked.

He stroked her cheek with his thumb and she felt her temperature rising. She would prove it to him. She rolled away from him and pulled him toward her. When he hesitated she touched his face. "Trust me."

He moved with her instruction until his body covered hers. She arched up against him and he slipped an arm under her back. He gasped out loud when she slipped her hand between them and guided him inside her. Nothing in his life could have prepared for the rush of intoxicating pleasure coursing through him. He held perfectly still, praying for control, but Callie had other plans. She moved under him once. At first he thought she wanted him to roll off, but when he moved, she moved her hands to his buttocks and held him. She dug her fingernails lightly into his skin and he pushed against her.

"See, that didn't hurt." She squeezed again.

"Woman, you don't know what you're doing." His breath shot out and he struggled for another.

"Do you like it?" she asked playfully.

"I've never felt anything like this."

"Like this?" She pushed up against him and took him fully inside her.

"Callie!" A spasm shot through him and he knew he couldn't last much longer. He had to please her; he couldn't let her down. Hoping he had the strength he began rocking against her.

With each stroke inside her, she grew more abandoned, her heart beating against his and her hands stroking his back and sides.

He lowered his head and took her nipple in his mouth. She arched hard up against him and cried out. Total bliss shook him when her sweetness contracted around him and she whispered his name over and over. Her body shook and trembled under him and she clung to him. He lowered his head down and brushed her cheek with his. Fear! He pulled away and brought the moisture of her tears away with him. "Callie, did I hurt you?"

"Oh Patric, let me show you how you hurt me."

She wrapped her legs around him and pushed against him until his mind went blank of everything except the feel of her around him. The beat of his heart reached the point of unbearable, and he stroked for release. He stopped breathing when she reached down and caressed him. Flashes of light shot through his head. Unable to hold himself back any longer, he groaned with sheer ecstasy, and collapsed on top of her. She kissed his cheeks, and again tears wet his face, but they didn't scare him this time.

"Beautiful."

"Yes, you are, Callie. More beautiful than words," he whispered before falling asleep on top of her.

She kissed his forehead and sighed. "Sweet dreams, my tortured hero."

Callie drifted off to sleep, holding him against her for dear life.

CHAPTER EIGHT

Patric stretched his muscles as he slipped awake. Sunlight streamed down onto his face and warmed him. He liked it. How many times had he cursed the blasted nurses for letting the sunshine in? His mind pulled up a dream, fantasies of Callie. Feeling well-rested, he wished he could dream like that all the time; it did wonders for his insomnia.

As he came more fully awake, he sensed something was wrong. No, not wrong, only different. The smell, the musty and stale smell of his room, didn't make him wrinkle his nose in disgust. Instead he was reminded of roses.

A second later the bed shifted and an arm flopped over his chest. Every part of his body tightened. He lifted his arm and touched her. *Callie!* His mind screamed. They'd really made love. How could that be? He'd come in and found her crying and then—

"What time is it?" Her voice wrapped around him with its sleepy undertones.

"And I would know this how?"

She bolted upright. "Oh, sorry!"

Patric had to laugh. "I'll say. I wasn't sure where I was when I woke up."

"Oh," she said a little more calmly.

"Callie, are you all right?" He reached out for her, and smiled when she took his hand. She turned his palm up and kissed it, letting her tongue dart out. The tightening in his mid-section increased and his hand shook. "Oh," he moaned.

She leaned over him and her bare chest brushed against his. He grabbed her and pulled her on top of him. She let out a startled gasp, then let herself relax. For a brief moment she thought he hadmeant to hurt her, but when she looked at Patric's face she remembered the previous night. His touch and his concern for her well-being, and her son's.

"Cameron." Where was he and why hadn't he come and woken her up? "I have to get my son breakfast."

He held her gently against him. "After breakfast can we call my attorney and see what can be done about this mess."

"Is it absolutely necessary to see a lawyer because we made love?"

Patric laughed. A rich deep laugh. "You are wicked. I meant about Cameron. I don't want to wait. It will give your ex a head start we can't afford."

Her heart burst with love for the man who, in spite of his own troubles, offered her support and the help she so desperately needed. "Are you sure?"

"This is the first thing in my life I've ever been sure of. Let me help you and Cam."

It sounded so natural for this man to call her son by her pet name. Being with him gave her strength and she would need all of it she could muster to fight Jason.

She pressed her lips against his and allowed him access into her mouth. His soft whimpers tickled her heartstrings and she smiled.

"Why are you smiling?"

She pulled away from him. "How did you know—"

"I feel it." He raised his hand and touched her lips. "Here, on you mouth, and in your breath."

"That's not fair. You're cheating." She kissed his fingers and pressed them to her cheek. "But I like the way you do it."

"What's a man have to do to get a meal around here?"

"You can start by letting me out of bed."

He pulled her down again and laughed into her neck. "Then I'll have to starve."

"But my son can't." She kissed him quickly and rolled off the bed before he could stop her.

"Twenty minutes. Be there."

"Yes, boss."

Patric lay in Callie's bed thinking. He never would have imagined he could feel these things. He'd never been taught to love and he didn't know if he could. Memories of his parents' violent arguments flashed through his mind. How he hated the way his father treated her. No one deserved such anger, and yet he'd inherited that anger and it had suffocated everyone who came near him. Even Callie, but still she had stayed.

He sat up and used his foot to locate his pants. He shivered with desire as he recalled how she'd taken them off. He sat back down and took a deep breath. How had she managed to get past his defenses? Thank God she had.

An hour later, he waited in the study for Callie to join him. They'd called the attorney and scheduled an appointment to meet with him. Patric laughed at Culpen's stuttering response to the news that the "dark prince" was coming into town. He'd almost choked. Then again so had he when Callie told him he had to go with her.

She didn't want to be alone if she got bad news.

Callie stepped into the room and stared awestruck at the magnificence of the man before her. He'd shaved himself completely, and managed to find a pressed pair of dress pants and a matching shirt. The navy blue cotton slacks hung loosely around his thighs, and the thin striped shirt pulled across his broad chest. He cleaned up splendidly, with only one flaw. She stepped up and began unbuttoning his shirt. His hands stopped her.

"Stop that. We are going to see Culpen, and no backing out."

"Hush up and stop flattering yourself," she teased. "You missed a button hole and I'm fixing it."

"Well, color me stupid."

"It really won't match the outfit. Blue is your color." She rebuttoned his shirt and wrapped her arms around his back. "Thank you."

He hugged her back. "For what?"

"Just thank you." She kissed him a moment before Cameron ran into the room.

"Let's go. I wanna see Jeremy."

His excitement about seeing his old school mate took some of the guilt out of her keeping this secret from him. She wanted to know what her chances were before she worried him.

The drive into town took less time than she expected and they dropped Cameron off at his friend's house in enough time to stop and get a *latte*. Patric stared straight ahead as they sat at an outside table across from the attorney's office building they would be going into.

"Are people staring at me?" He fiddled with his cup and almost spilled it several times.

Callie knew how hard this had to be for him, and she

shared his discomfort. "No, darlin'. Only a petite blonde woman who is beginning to grow annoyed at your obvious lack of interest in her fluttering eyelashes."

"Don't make fun of me, Callie." He started to pull away from her.

"I'm not. She's been staring at you since she got here."

"Cut it out, Callie, it's not funny." Patric fidgeted with his cup and fumbled for the spoon on the table.

Callie pushed away the momentary twinge of guilt and set out on her mission, hoping it would not backfire in her face. She leaned to the side and signaled the blonde woman a few tables away. "I'm sorry, I couldn't help notice you seem to have an interest in my friend. Would you like me to introduce you?"

"Well, if you don't mind." Her sultry voice slipped through the air and slammed against Callie's patience. "I've been wondering if a man that handsome can be as friendly."

She saw Patric's face blush, but he didn't move. "I'll get you for this."

When the woman stood up and sashayed toward them Callie thanked the stars Patric couldn't see her. "Patric LeClerc, this is—"

"Carlisle Parker, but my friends call me Carlie."

Callie choked on her water when she heard the woman's name. Ms. Parker held the distinction of being one of New Orleans most sought-after socialites. The Parker family held the largest financial grip on the city. "I'm Callie Carpenter. I'm Mr. LeClerc's—"

"Girlfriend," Patric finished. "Callie and I live together."

Callie's mouth fell open so wide she could have

crawled in. A second later someone's foot bumped against her chair then slipped up her leg. Since Ms. Parker stood upright she assumed it had to be Patric's foot.

"I'm sorry, I didn't realize." The woman took a step back. "Wait, are you the LeClerc who lives up at Garden View?"

"It's Dark Gardens, and yes I am."

"Well, goodness. I'd heard you'd been horribly scarred in some kind of accident years back."

Callie scooted forward on her seat. "As you can see—"

"You're not so terribly scarred. In fact..." her voice trailed off as her hand moved up toward his cheek. "You're quite—"

"Handsome," Callie finished. "Yes, I think so too."

Carlisle Parker's hand dropped down to her side and she smiled sweetly down at Patric. Her heavy lashed lowered over her sparkling blue eyes and the corner of her lip curled up into a seductive smile. She leaned forward, offering everyone near a blazing view of her obviously expensive cleavage and looked straight into Patric's face.

Callie stifled a laugh. The flaming hussy had no idea the man she ogled couldn't see her. Blind as a bat. "Patric, dear, it's time we headed to our appointment. Let me take care of the check and we'll get going."

"Callie, I'll get it." He pulled his wallet out of his back pocket and fumbled for the bills tucked inside. He pulled out a ten-dollar bill and held it out in front of him.

Callie watched Carlisle's expression when he waved the bill slightly off sides. Callie plucked it out of his hand and signaled the waiter.

"Why hasn't he looked at me?" The irritation in Ms.

Parker's voice grated on Callie's nerves.

"Because, Ms. Parker, I'm stone-blind."

Her mouth dropped open so wide that Callie swore everyone in the place could have climbed in. She expected some reaction, but not this.

"You mean I've been standing here talking to a—a—blind man." She rubbed her arms vigorously. "He can't even see—me."

"No, I can't, but I can hear you."

"We have to go Patric." Callie stood up and took his arm. She smiled at their new acquaintance and they walked away.

"You are a wicked woman, Callie Carpenter, and if you ever do that to me again—you're fired."

"Oh, am I now? And who else will put up with your bad attitude?" Callie stopped and looked at him. "Patric, I'm—"

"It's okay. I know what you meant, and you're right. I guess I should apologize."

Callie led him through the handicap door, opting against the revolving one. Her heels clicked on the floor as she led them to the elevator. She grabbed Patric's arm when the toe of his shoe caught on the plush carpet of the cubicle floor. She pushed the button and the elevator moved slowly. The door opened and they stepped directly into the reception area of Maitlin Culpen's law office. The deep burgundy carpet lay thick under her feet and the hunter green paisley printed walls screamed of masculinity.

A tight-skinned sleekly coifed woman of about thirty sat behind a mahogany desk. She dropped her pen when she looked up and saw Patric. She slipped her glasses off and stood. "Patric, I mean Mr. LeClerc. I didn't think you—"

"Sandra. It's been quite a few years." He held out his hand and she took it.

"How did you know it was me?" She put her hand up to her chin after he let it go.

"You still wear the same perfume and you have a distinctive voice."

Callie stepped forward and interrupted the reunion. She forced herself to ignore her second twinge of jealousy in less than an hour. Not a habit she wanted to get into. "We have an appointment with Mr. Culpen."

Sandra skimmed the desk log and looked up apologetically. "You're name isn't on here, Pat—Mr."

"It's Ms. Carpenter." Callie had the distinct feeling she didn't exist. "It's about an upcoming custody hearing." Waves of every imaginable emotion washed over her. Her jealousy of the women openly flirting with Patric was quickly pushed aside by the fear of losing Cameron.

"Oh—my—goodness. You're the one who is going up against the Carpenter family."

Callie's patience snapped and the enormity of the situation overwhelmed her. "I am part of the Carpenter family, whether I want to be or not. I have no intention of letting them take my son away, so if you could tell Mr. Culpen I'm here so I can get on with my life."

"Callie, calm down."

She spun around and faced Patric. How dare he tell her to calm down? She could lose her only child at any given moment and all he had time to do was flirt with old flames. He had obviously had an affair with Sandra at some point and Callie couldn't help wondering when. "Don't!"

The door behind the front desk opened and a tall gangly man stepped out. "I'm Maitlin Culpen." He looked past her. "Patric, are my eyes deceiving me, or are you out of the mausoleum?"

"It's me, in the flesh. I'd like to say you haven't changed a bit, but—"

"And you seem to have acquired a sense of humor over the years."

Patric smiled. "Must be the company I'm keeping."

"Can we get on with this? My son's future and my life depend on it."

Both men turned to her and Callie grinned sheepishly. "Sorry, I guess I'm a little bit anxious." She followed Culpen into his office.

Two hours later, Callie wrapped her arms around her son and held him like she'd never done before. After a few minutes he pulled out of her embrace and slipped back into his seat next to her. She held the ignition key for a moment then lowered her head to rest on the steering wheel.

"Mom, what's wrong?" Cameron's small voice quivered as he stared at his mom.

"We have to talk about something. I don't want you to be scared, but there might be some changes in our lives."

"Are we gonna have to move again?" Callie frowned when he turned his attention to Patric. "Are you making my mom lose her job again?"

"Oh, Cameron, this isn't Patric's fault. He's helping us." She reached out and touched Patric's cheek. A growth of stubble already covered his face. She remembered the feel of his skin against hers and sighed.

"Remember when I told you I would never let your father take you away from me?" Callie watched his features melt into fear.

"You've changed your mind. You don't want me anymore?"

Callie swept him into her arms and she held him tight. "Oh, baby, of course I want you. You're my whole life. I'd be lost without you."

"Then why are you making me go away?" Tears rolled down his cheeks and Callie's heart broke.

"Cam, you're not going anywhere. Let your mother explain." Patric reached up and felt for the back of the seat.

"Patric and I have just been to see an attorney and he says that the only way to keep you is to let your father see you sometimes."

His small shoulder began to tremble and Callie reached out to him.

"So, I have to go?" His voice cracked and his whimpers turned into sobs.

"Honey, I don't know. I don't want you to worry about this. Mr. Culpen says I might have to let you visit so Jason won't take you away from me."

"Cameron, I'm not going to let Jason take you away from your mom. I swear."

"Let's go home and spend some time together."

Callie gave her son a quick hug and started the car. They rode back to the house in complete silence. Cameron stared blindly out the car window and never looked in her direction.

Cameron ran into the house and up to his room before Callie could catch up with him. She watched him disappear and the slam of his door echoed through the silent house. "I have to go make him understand."

"Callie, I don't know much about kids, but I remember how I was at his age."

"You were a kid once?" She tried to lighten things up, but he didn't allow it.

"Callie, let him go for a while. I think you both need some time to think about all this." Patric made his way carefully down the hallway and into the study.

Callie followed and watched him fumble with a bottle of seltzer water. Once he'd poured the water up to his finger he capped the remainder and turned around. His eyes stared directly at her and for a brief second she believed he could actually see her. What would she give for that to be true?

Patric stood, amazed. The light behind Callie cast a shadow and he could see her silhouette. He took several steps toward her and reached out. The closer he got, the less visible the shadow grew. "Callie, I wish I could do more. All I can do is promise to be with you through all of this."

"That means a lot to me. The entire time I was married to Jason I prayed I wouldn't have to be alone. He never had time to do anything—except hurt me."

He held out his arms and Callie stepped into his embrace. Her head rested on his chest and he took the opportunity to stroke her hair. The silky strands wound around his fingers and fell down around her face. He moved his finger and pushed the hair back, brushing it against her cheek. Soft didn't begin to describe her skin. His stomach flopped when she sighed. He pushed her away, but she held fast.

"Please hold me. I don't think I can stand another rejection." Her tears fell onto his chest.

His head tipped back and he fought against the desire racing through his veins. "I'm not rejecting you. I couldn't if I wanted to, and I don't." He wrapped her in his embrace as tightly as he could without crushing her. "I just want this to be us, not grief."

She lifted her head and brushed her lips across his. "This is us. It has been from the beginning. I know you don't believe me, but I have never been so—entranced by anyone."

"Are you sure this has nothing to do with the way your ex treated you?"

Her head fell back onto his chest and her breathing evened out. "This has everything to do with Jason."

"I knew it." He pulled away from her and moved toward the couch. He edged back onto the closest end and sat. The cushion of the seat pressed against his thighs and he shifted uncomfortably. He groaned inwardly when Callie sat next to him. Her hand touched his arm and he trembled. The slightest contact between them intoxicated him to the point of incoherence.

"I can't deal with that."

"Patric, you don't understand."

"I don't have to." He leaned against the arm of the couch, but she moved closer.

"Patric, I know the difference between you and Jason. He went out of his way to hurt me. The only time Jason and I were together was when he forced me. And if I argued, he--beat me."

"God, Callie." Ice rolled through him and his fists clenched in his lap. Blazing fury soon replaced the cold anger coursing through him. Then reality numbed him. What the hell could he do about it? Jason had everything a man needed and could see the enemy. Patric lowered his head in defeat. He couldn't see anything.

"For the first time in my life I know what I want."

Callie reached out for him.

"No. You deserve better."

Patric stood and walked away. He swore out loud as his knee smashed against a small table just before exiting the room. He fought against his need to go back and comfort her when her sobs reached his ears.

Callie listened as he stomped up the stairs. She didn't have to guess where he was going. When things didn't go his way he went to his weight room. She had to go after him, but had no idea what to say to him. Why couldn't he see he was more than good enough for her?

"For God's sake, you're blind, not worthless." Her voice echoed out across the room. *What do I have to do to prove how much I love you?* "That's it!" She bounced out of her seat and headed for the telephone, all thoughts of her own problems vanishing with her idea.

Callie spent the entire afternoon on the telephone asking questions. When she finally disconnected from the last call, she hugged herself and went in search of Patric. She knocked on his bedroom door, thinking it had been too long for him to still be working out. When he didn't answer she headed down the hall.

"Patric?" She pushed the door open and found him on the weight bench with a barbell hanging over his chest. "I need to talk to you."

"Go away." His breath hissed out as he lowered then lifted the weight. His chest heaved and his muscles bulged.

Callie watched the fluid motion of his arms as he repeated the motions. She'd never watched a man exercise before, and her arousal at the sight amazed her. "Please," she whispered.

"I'm busy."

"Like this can't wait. How long have you been doing this, any way?"

Patric settled the bar in the braces and let his arms dangle beside him. "I don't see it's any of your business." He inched forward and reached up to shield his head from the bar.

"Patric. I have to tell you something, and I don't want to wait."

He let out a sigh and turned toward her. "Fine, spit it out."

She walked toward him and placed her hand on his chest. He trembled before backing away. His legs bumped against another machine and he rotated and took a seat. She watched him loop his cotton-clad legs behind a bar and begin lifting the weights with his legs. He exhaled slowly and lifted again.

"Callie, what do you want?"

"I want to help you." She took a step forward, but his frown stopped her.

"You do. You get paid to take care of me and you do that just fine. Now, if there's nothing else."

"There is. I was thinking about what you said earlier and I think I know how I can help you."

CHAPTER NINE

Patric replayed their conversations from earlier in the day and came up with no clue as to what she was talking about. His legs screamed in pain as he lifted the weight yet again. He'd done twice his normal workout before she'd come in and now he was forcing a third time on his aching muscles. He'd sat on the sofa downstairs wanting her so badly it hurt, and all she could do was compare him to her monster of an ex. The pain of his blindness didn't hold a candle to the searing agony of her lack of desire for him.

"Are you listening, Patric?"

He sighed and blew out a deep breath. I'm blind, not deaf."

"I made some calls and spoke with a few doctor friends and I found out that there is a clinic in Texas that does experimental research and surgery on willing participants."

"What the hell are you talking about?"

"Patric, they have a procedure that allows them to replace damaged eyes with new ones. It has something to do with an artificial retina."

"Good Lord!" he shouted.

"Don't you see? You could get your sight back, or at least some of it."

He jerked his legs free and stood. "Come here." He kept his voice low and controlled until she brushed against him. When her chest touched his, he reached for her arms. As gently as his fury would allow, he held her. "Don't you ever take it upon yourself to make decisions like that on my behalf."

"Patric, you're scaring me." She pulled out of his grasp and he let her.

"I have discussed every damn operation known to mankind concerning eyes and I didn't find one that could do me a damn bit of good."

"This is new and they have only done it a few times, with minimal success."

"And you want to set me up for a boat load of pain and disappointment?" he snorted. "Thanks for the concern."

"You don't understand. They've made some breakthrough discoveries and all they need are patients to test them on."

"I can't believe you. Get the hell out, and don't do me any favors."

He listened for her retreating footsteps, but she didn't move. "Go!" The harshness of his own voice scared him.

A second later, she ran out of the room. Misery swept through him, hot and fast. His chest tightened and he crumpled to the floor. How many doctors had he talked to? How many had been a waste of time? One disappointment after another had led him to this very place. Every no, every rejection, every dismissal had stripped another chunk of his desire to care. He refused to put Callie and Cameron through the same torture. He'd rather die alone and blind, than make them live those nightmares.

Tears rolled down his cheeks and he shivered when they fell onto his bare chest. The warmth reminded him of how Callie's tears had followed the same trail. He smelled her rose perfume several minutes before she spoke.

"I suppose you want me to pack my life up and get out of your way."

Her voice shook and he needed to hold her, to tell her he loved her and couldn't hurt her that way. He wanted to look into her eyes and apologize. He wanted to see her, but he couldn't and he never would. He raised himself up off the floor.

"Callie, this has nothing to do with your job. You're good at what you do and I need—your skills." He swallowed hard and turned away from her.

"That's all? You have nothing else to say?"

"I want you and Cameron to stay here at Dark Gardens and I want to continue to help you with your custody battle, but my personal life is off limits." He listened as Callie paced the room several times. Finally, she stopped. Her breath blew across his shoulder and he stopped breathing.

"Yes, sir." And she left. When she did, every ounce of hope he'd had went with her.

He stumbled to his room and struggled with the shower. The steaming water rolled off his back and down the drain. Drop by drop, his strength dissipated and followed it. For the first time in his pathetic life he'd experienced a flicker of the ever-elusive emotion he'd been robbed of. He'd loved, and for a brief moment in time, he'd imagined he could be loved. He shook his head and lifted his face to the spray of water.

Two weeks passed with little conversation between Callie and Patric. To Callie's dismay, Cameron spent most of his time wandering the estate grounds. Every time she tried to talk to him, he turned away and mumbled something about being fine. On the day before his first scheduled visit with his father, Callie made him stop and talk to her.

"Cam, we need to discuss this." She cupped his cheek with her trembling hand and looked into her son's soft hazel eyes. "I know you're mad at me, but we have to get this cleared up before your visit."

Cameron fidgeted out of her reach and started up the stairs. "I'm not mad. I'm gonna go pack."

Callie's patience snapped and she ran up the stairs after him. "No! You are not going to pack, because you aren't going anywhere." Callie spun around when she heard Patric's voice.

"Callie, I think you should be—"

Her hair caught in her mouth and she sputtered as she tried to spit it out. "Stay out of this. You set the rules, no personal interference, and I am his mother, which makes him my personal business. No one is taking my son away from me." Tears streamed down her cheeks as she turned back to her son. Cameron stood at the top of the stairs staring down at her.

"Mom, why are you yelling at Patric? You're the one who's letting me go." He ran down the hall and slammed his door behind him.

Callie collapsed on the stairs and cradled her head in her hands. "Why won't he listen to me? What is it about the male species that won't allow them to listen to women?"

"I don't know the answer to that, but maybe I can help."

"How's that?" Callie stood up and walked toward him. Her hand brushed against the rosewood banister and the coolness of the wood soothed her, but only a little.

"I know how he feels. I remember when I got sent off to school. I hated both my parents for making me go away."

"But I don't want him to go. You know that."

Patric held out his hand and Callie grasped it. The tension between them evaporated as their hands met. Callie enjoyed the feel of his palm against hers and she needed his strength right now.

Patric pulled his hand away. "Would you mind if I tried to talk to him, man to man?"

Callie immediately missed the warmth and wished they hadn't spent so much time arguing and avoiding one another. "I have to go and tell him I love him, then you can talk to him."

"Callie, I know how hard this must be for you, but everything will work out for the best. I promise."

"Nothing about my son being with that beast can be good."

She paced back and forth several times before stopping to stare at the man before her. How far he'd come since her arrival amazed her. He had grown from an insensitive beast to a man unconcerned for his own self. He'd taken Cameron under his wing and the two had become genuine friends. She imagined what life would be like if she stayed with Patric. She pushed the thought away. No matter how well he got along with her son, Patric would never love her.

"Callie, you and Cameron will be fine. I know you aren't planning on staying here forever, but when you are gone, Cameron will readjust and he'll get used to his new home."

Cameron stood at the top of the stairs in an alcove listening to his mother talk about him. She wasn't even sad about him leaving, and how could she even think about leaving Patric? He needed them. Cameron wouldn't leave the only man who'd ever treated him like a man. He loved Patric and he'd find a way to stay, whether his mother wanted him or not.

He tiptoed down the hallway and crept down the back stairs. Before running out the kitchen door, he grabbed a bag of chips and several pre-made sandwiches his mother always kept in the refrigerator in case Patric got hungry in the middle of the night.

He stepped outside and looked around the yard. The clouds partially covered the moon and gave off an eerie light. Cameron shivered. *No, I can't be scared.* He tripped over the broom and set it back up against the wall before running down the path into the forest. He'd hide until it was too late for his father to come get him. Then he'd make Patric keep him.

Callie ran through the house, from room to room, screaming Cameron's name. She jerked open door after door searching for her son. When she reached Patric's door, she shoved it open without hesitation. She looked around the empty room, praying for a sign of her child. When none appeared, she sank to the floor on her knees, crying out in desperation. Sobs of frustration shook her entire body, over and over, until she could no longer hold herself upright. Blinding fear consumed her as she crumbled.

Patric stumbled into the room and bumped into Callie's trembling body. He immediately kneeled down and wrapped his arms around her. The warmth of her tears soaked through his shirt and her pain burned into his heart. "What's happened?"

She clutched his shoulders and her tongue stumbled over the words she desperately struggled to voice. "Cam—he's—my fault—gone." She began crying again.

Warning sirens went off in his head and he willed himself to remain calm. He stroked her hair and rocked her gently. "Tell me what happened."

"No time. He's run away." She grabbed at his shirt. "I can't lose him."

Patric rubbed his fingertips along her shoulders, urging her to relax. "Baby, I'll fix it, but you have to calm down and be ready when he gets home. Can you do that?"

"He's all I have, I can't lose him." She stared up at him, tears streaking down her cheeks.

Patric held her face between his hands and rested his forehead against hers. Once she'd stopped crying, he helped her up and settled her on the edge of the bed. "Call the police and tell them what's happened."

He waited until she was talking to someone before he carefully made his way down the stairs and to the kitchen door.

The evening humidity wrapped around him as he stepped out onto the porch. He didn't have any idea what he was going to do, but he had to do something. The memory of Callie's voice shaking as she described her missing son to the officer on the telephone rattled him into action. His heart raced as he felt along the wall for the broom he remembered bumping into earlier in the day. When his hand struck the handle he grabbed it up and headed off across the yard. After the bristles brushed against his face several times, he broke the end of the broom off in frustration. He tossed the bundled straw aside and kept walking.

"Cameron, I know you're out here. Your mom is really worried about you." He stood still listening for signs of the boy, but even his sensitized hearing failed to detect anything. He made his way through several small bushes, nearly falling twice. He prayed he would be able to find Cameron soon, or he'd never find his way back to the house. He should have considered this problem before wandering off into the forest by himself.

"Come on, Cam, I need you to come out. If you don't come out I'll never get home. I need you, Cam."

Patric heard a noise behind him and swung around toward it. His foot caught on something and he fell. His head hit the trunk of a nearby tree and he blinked twice.

Cameron came out of the bushes and ran toward Patric's fallen body. He knelt down and shook the large man. "Patric, wake up. I'm here. We can go home now."

But Patric didn't move.

Cameron grabbed his shirt and shook him several times. Patric's head rolled to the side just as the moon came into full view. Tears sprang from Cameron's eyes when a stream of blood rolled down Patric's face.

"I'm sorry, Patric. I didn't mean for you to get hurt." Cameron cradled Patric's head in his lap and cried. After a few minutes he remembered something his mother had said once.

"Never let your fear be stronger than your heart. You have to protect the ones you love at any cost."

She'd told him that right after his first fight. He loved Patric, and yes, he was as scared as he'd ever been, but he had to be strong and get help. He settled Patric's head back onto the grass and got up. He looked own and wiped the tears off his cheek. "I'll get help for you and then mom will see I'm a man and should decide by myself where I wanna live."

Callie stood in front of the house looking around. Two officers checked out the yard and two others stood next to their squad car. She'd give anything to have Cameron back. She needed to feel her son in her arms. She watched as another car drove up the driveway. Her stomach churned as Jason stepped out of the small sports car.
"So, you managed to lose my son, did you?"
"Not now, Jason." She turned her back on him and scanned the forest edge.
He grabbed her by the arm and flung her around to face him. "Yes, now!" he barked. "This is very clever, but it won't work. If you think I am stupid enough to believe that the kid would run away, you're dead wrong."
"You don't have any idea what my son is capable of. You don't know and you don't care. You never have."
A police officer stepped between them and laid his hand on Jason's arm. "Step back, sir."
"No, I want this woman arrested. Now!"
"What exactly would you like me to arrest her for?"
Jason glared at the man before turning back to Callie. "Kidnapping."
"*What?*" Callie and the officer spoke at the same time.
"We are in the middle of a custody battle and this is

her sick and twisted way of keeping me from my son. I won't stand for it."

"You what? He's not your son. You've never given a damn about Cameron, and I don't need to kidnap him. No judge in his right mind would give a child to a monster like you."

"Careful what you say, Callie. All of this will be public record, and I'd hate for you to offend the judge before the hearing. How do you think Judge Harkins will react when I tell him you said he couldn't be objective, just because he grew up with my daddy. That couldn't be good for your case."

Callie stepped back from the menace in his voice and digested his veiled threat. She opened her mouth to tell him where he could shove his threat when she heard Cameron screaming from behind the house. She broke away from the group and ran hell-bent toward his voice. "Cameron!"

"Mom, Patric is hurt! He fell and I couldn't get him to wake up. I'm scared I kilt him."

Callie held her son against her chest as his sobs shook them both. "Calm down, honey. Tell me where he is and we'll go get him." She listened as her son gave sketchy directions on how to find Patric.

Jason reached them seconds before the police officers and grabbed Cameron away from her. Fear swept through her, but was quickly replaced with a maternal instinct to protect her son, no matter what.

Without thought, she reached out and grabbed Jason's arm. "Get your hand off my son, you bastard."

The sting of his hand across her face fueled her anger, and for the first time in her life she hauled off and slapped him back. Hard. Pain shot up her arm as she hit him again, and her palm throbbed from the impact.

"Stop it!" Cameron yelled. "We have to save Patric! He needs me."

A burly officer pulled Jason back and allowed Cameron to retell his story.

The officer in charge pulled his radio and verified that a paramedic unit had been dispatched. Cameron stood by his mother and repeated his directions to the police officer, but in the end, he demanded to be allowed to help in the rescue.

Patric still lay unconscious when Cameron ran up next to him. He grabbed his hand and mumbled to him.

Callie knelt down, but the paramedics found them and pushed her aside. Several police officers carrying large lanterns surrounded them as the medics gave Patric a quick check over.

After relaying vital signs and information to the hospital over the radio, they lifted him onto a hand-held stretcher and carried him out of the woods. Unable to do anything else, Callie followed along, her sobbing son in tow.

Less than an hour later she found herself pacing the hospital waiting-room. She wanted—no, *needed* to see Patric. She had to know he would be all right. She turned to find Doctor Jameson coming down the hall. She had called him about the experimental surgery for Patric's eyes.

"Callie, I don't know what your relationship with Mr. LeClerc is, but this head trauma has done some damage. I am going to run some tests, but I'm sure that under the circumstances there is a fifty-fifty chance the surgery could be successful in restoring some, if not all, of his vision. All I need is a signature on the consent form."

Callie sat down on the nearest chair and stared off into space. Patric had made his thoughts on the subject very clear, but how could she not give him the opportunity to see again? She stood back up and began pacing. She brushed her fingers through her hair and turned to face the doctor. During their first visit to the attorney, Patric had surprised her by giving her the power to make decisions on his behalf in an emergency. Could she abuse that trust he'd put in her?

She squared her shoulders. "I've made my decision."

Patric woke to a tremendous pounding in his temple. He instinctively reached over to his bedside table and searched for the pain pills. Then he remembered, he hadn't used the pain pills since...

"Callie?" He rolled his head to the side and searing pain shot through his head and down into his neck. One by one memories flooded back into his mind and crowded his head. He'd gone out to find Cameron and had fallen. Everything else remained fuzzy, like where he was. He groped for the pill bottle, but couldn't even find the blasted table. "Callie?"

He heard something next to him and then her hand was on his chest. "Lay still, Patric. You're in the hospital and you need to be still."

"Callie, is Cameron all right? I tried to find him, but couldn't."

"I know. It's okay. Cameron is out in the waiting room with one of the nurses. He saw you fall and came to get help."

Patric sighed. He'd gone out to find Cameron and the little man had rescued him. "That's quite a boy you have there."

Callie squeezed his hand and he returned the gesture.

"Patric, I need to tell you something."

"Are you sure Cam is all right?"

Yes, he's fine. I was given a consent form to authorize the surgery I told you about."

He jerked his hand away from her. "I trusted you not to abuse your power."

"Please listen to me. I'm trying to explain to you. I wanted so much for you to be able to see. I knew if you could you would see how wonderful we could all be together, as a family." The agony of his mistrust set her emotions on end. How could he be so unwilling to even hear her out?

"Damn you, Callie, I told you how I felt. I thought after our talk you had realized I don't want any part of it."

Callie reached for his hand, but he pulled away. "You don't understand."

"No, you don't understand. I told you no. I specifically told you I was not willing to take that chance and you do this." He turned his head away from her and let the pain take him away.

Callie stood staring down at him. Ironically, tears blinded her and his image blurred and disappeared when she closed her eyes against the salty burn. He hadn't even listened to her.

He'd only assumed she would ignore his feelings entirely. She stepped back away from the bed and left the room. Without a word she took Cameron, who'd been waiting outside the door, and they left the hospital. He rambled to her the entire way back to Dark Garden, but she remained silent.

When they pulled into the winding drive Cameron stomped his foot on the car floor. "I'm not a baby."

Callie looked over at him. " I know."

"Then why won't you tell me what's wrong?"

He glared over at her and she wished with all her heart she could tell him. But how would she explain to her child that she loved a man and planned to walk out of that very same man's life without so much as a good-bye? She didn't understand it herself.

"Is this my fault?"

"Oh, Cameron, of course it isn't your fault."

She reached over to touch him, but he pushed her hand away. "Please. I can't worry about Patric right now. You are my only concern. I have to find a way to keep your father from taking you away."

She pulled the car up in front of the house and urged Cameron out. She pulled the back seat down. Her only choice was to leave. Patric didn't trust her, didn't care for her, and she couldn't live like that. "Cameron, I want you to go upstairs and get all your things together."

"Mom, I don't want to go. I like it here."

Cameron scuffed the toe of his shoe along in the dust. Instead of going in the house he plopped down on the lowest step leading into the house. "Can't you fix it? Make it better?"

Callie sat next to him and put her arm around his shoulder. "Honey, I wish I could."

Cameron picked up a pebble off the step and tossed it across the yard. He turned and faced Callie. "I thought Patric loved us. I mean—well—this is the same thing dad did to us."

Callie pulled him against her and hugged him as

tightly as he would allow. "No, Cam, Patric did—does care about us, but he has too many things he needs to figure out on his own. I don't want us to be in the way."

"How could we be in the way if he loves us."

Callie sniffed back the tears. She didn't want him to see her cry again. "Cam, we can talk about this another time. Right now we need to get our things and find a place to stay." Callie stood and held out her hand to Cameron. He took it and together they walked into the house.

An hour later they pulled away from Dark Gardens. She looked down at the folded newspaper and prayed she would find them an apartment she could afford on what she'd saved.

CHAPTER TEN

Patric lay in his hospital bed and waited. He'd done the very same thing for fifteen days, and every night, he had fallen asleep frustrated. Callie had not been back to see him since their argument. No, they hadn't argued. He'd insulted her and doubted her faith in him. How could he justify that? He had no faith in himself. Why should she? Did she even know he would go home today? Would she even care?

"Mr. LeClerc, your ride home is here and all of your discharge papers are in order. You're free to go."

"Must be my lucky day. I'm free to go and don't have any place to be." Patric listened to the people moving around him and searched for some chord of familiarity.

"Patric, are you ready?"

He smelled Sandra's perfume a second before hearing her voice. "Mr. Culpen sent me to take you back to the house."

"Wonderful. What more could I possibly need?"

Patric stood and Sandra turned him so he could relocate himself into the customary wheelchair. His head hung low as she wheeled him out into the humid afternoon. His heart raced for a moment. Would Callie be at the house waiting for him? Probably not.

"Can I ask you something?" Sandra's voice interrupted his thoughts.

"By all means. My life is an open book."

"It's about that. Why do you do that?" Sandra slowed down and lowered the front wheels of the chair down off the sidewalk.

"Why do I do what?" he grunted.

The chair stopped rolling. "You are one of the grumpiest people I have ever met. You snap and yell at every person who comes near you."

"You know what, Sandy? Maybe you could mind your own damn business."

Patrick slammed his hands down onto the rolling wheels and grunted when the rubber scraped against his palm. "Damn!"

"Cut it out. Or I'll take you right back inside and leave you there." Sandy stopped the chair and moved around in front of him.

Her breath blew across his cheek and he thought of Callie. Her tender lips, her soft rose scent, and the feel of her body pressed against his. "What do I care. I don't have anything to go back there for."

"What about Callie—I mean Ms. Carpenter?"

"Leave it alone."

"Oh, Patric. You didn't run her off too. Did you?"

Sandra caressed his cheek and her pity seeped into his soul.

"I mean it. My life is none of your business. You made that decision a long time ago."

"No, Patric, you did."

Patric raised his head and leaned forward until his face touched hers. "You walked out on me because you couldn't stand being tied down to an invalid."

She breathed a deep sigh. "When did I ever say that?"

"You didn't have to. You left. You packed up all

your stuff and you left without a word." His voice softened. "What was I suppose to think?"

His own loneliness overwhelmed him, and he leaned into her palm when she touched his cheek. Her fingers pushed up into his hair and he sighed. For the millionth time in two weeks his heart ached.

"Patric, you told me to leave, and then you locked yourself in your room. I stayed for two days."

"You didn't stay long enough." His head fell forward. "No one ever stays long enough."

"When did you last talk to her?"

"Who?" Patric asked blankly.

"You know who." The breath on his face disappeared and he heard Sandra move away. "Do you even know that her custody hearing is today at three o'clock?"

Patric's muscles tightened and his stomach threatened to spill the less than appetizing lunch he'd forced down earlier. How could Callie have not told him? He cared about her son as much as she did. The thought startled him. He loved Cameron. No matter how much he'd fought the feelings he couldn't ignore the fact that he loved someone. "I'm supposed to care?"

"Don't give me that crap. I know you too well, in spite of everything that happened between us. You are hopelessly in love with Callie Carpenter and her heartbreaker of a son."

"What do you want me to do about it? She hasn't bothered to come and see me since the night I ended up here at the Ritz."

"What did you do to her?"

She knew him better than he thought. "I guess I showed her the real me and she couldn't take it."

The heels of Sandra's shoes clicked on the sidewalk

in front of him. She paced back and forth a few times before moving behind his wheelchair and gave it a shove. "You are the most exasperating man I have ever met. I left you because you told me to. It would have happened eventually on its own—"

"Says who?"

"Shut up, and listen to me." She stopped the chair and her hand brushed his as she snapped the brake lever in place. "I know you aren't going to like this, but I can't stand the thought of you spending the rest of your life feeling sorry for yourself."

"Who appointed you my keeper?" Patric snapped as she shoved him forward out of the wheelchair. She covered the top of his head with her hand as he climbed into the front seat of her car.

"Don't push me, LeClerc. I am doing this for your own good and some day you'll thank me. One way or another."

She slammed his door and he waited for her to get in behind the wheel. The hair on his arms stood up and he knew she meant business. "So what exactly will I be thanking you for?" She didn't answer. "Sandra?"

"Be a good boy and ride nice."

Callie paced the length of her living room. She'd been pacing for nearly an hour. "Cameron, are you ready?" She stopped outside the door when he didn't answer. "Cam?"

"I'm not going." His voice trembled and her heart broke for the millionth time that day.

For a child he understood things too clearly. He knew he might not be coming home with her after the hearing. No matter how she tried, she couldn't find any words of encouragement. All she could do is cry. She should be nearly out of tears. "Please, honey."

"No! If I don't go they can't take me away."

She opened the door and her heart sank at the sight of all the clutter around the room. The apartment she'd rented barely held Cameron and her, much less their belongings, meager though they were. "It doesn't work that way, sweetheart. We have to let the judge decide."

"Mom, what if they make me go live with him?"

She rushed across the room and swept him up into her arms. His shoulders shook, but when she tilted his face up it was free of tears. "You are being so brave, and I'm so proud of you."

"I don't feel very brave. I'm scared."

Callie hugged him tighter. "Me too, Cam, but I promise you this. If that judge makes you go live with Jason, I'll fight with every breath in me to get you back. I won't stop until we're together."

"I don't want to live with them."

"I know, but promise me that if you have to you will behave until I can get you back."

"But—"

"No, promise me, Cameron. This is so important."

He lowered his head and rubbed his fingers across her hand. "I promise, mom. But if they take me away, you have to work super duper fast to make the judge give me back."

"Cross my heart." She drew a cross over her heart. He grabbed her hand and held it to his cheek. "Now, can you get dressed?"

"Yeah."

Callie stepped out into the front room and resumed her pacing. The small clock on the wall chimed two.

Cameron came out of his room and they left the apartment together in silence.

Outside the courtroom, Callie reminded Cameron about telling the truth, no matter what. They stepped into the courtroom and nausea threatened to overcome Callie as she faced her ex-husband. The sneer on his face told her all she needed to know. He would stop at nothing to destroy her. The custody battle wasn't about having a son as special as Cameron. It all hinged on his evil need to manipulate and control everything and everyone in his life. Jason didn't like to lose, and he would go to any length to get what he wanted. This week he wanted to buy a son for his child-bride. Next week, who knew?

The petite blond stood next to Jason and did what he intended her to do—look good. Isabel must look stunning in his trophy case, and driving his trophy cars and batting her well-mascared lashes to woo his many clients. Status meant the world to Jason, and Isabel held the position of main trophy, a position she herself had never quite filled to his satisfaction. But then, she hadn't ever wanted to be nothing but a trophy.

"Callie, don't you look—like you." Jason stepped toward her and leered down at her. His breath wreaked of whisky and his bloodshot eyes looked glassy.

"I can't believe you would come here drunk." Callie stepped back and fanned the invisible vapors away. His breath crept around her like a dense fog and her stomach lurched.

"I'm not drunk. I'm celebrating."

"I'm afraid to ask why." Callie could only imagine his excuse for such a display. She prayed the judge would notice Jason's intoxication and toss the custody case out.

Maitlin Culpen stepped up and placed his hand on Callie's shoulder. "Let's get settled."

"So, honey, how'd you manage to scrape up the bucks to pay for him, or is he taking it out in trade?"

Callie stepped forward and raised her hand, but her attorney grabbed it and pulled her toward the front of the courtroom. He urged her down into the dark wood chair and glared at her.

"Callie, have you lost your mind?"

"Did you hear what he said to me?" Callie swiveled around and stared at the hulking man she'd once been married to. Isabel clung to his arm and fawned over him like a prize poodle.

"Yes, Callie, I did hear. Do you have any idea how a judge would have seen the print of your hand on Jason's face? You might as well hand Cameron over to your ex on a silver platter."

The bailiff stepped into the room and a court reporter followed. They settled into their respective places and Callie waited for the judge. Mr. Culpin had called to give her the name of the judge several days earlier. She asked as many questions of old acquaintances as she could without being obvious, afraid of finding a connection between the judge and Jason's family.

When she came up empty, her fears subsided slightly.

Her heart stopped when the door behind the bench opened. A tall and brooding man emerged from the chamber and approached the high backed leather chair. He gazed around the room and his gaze rested on Isabel. The corner of his thin lip went up, but barely enough to notice. Isabel wiggled her finger at him and lowered her lashes. Callie watched the whole display with a dreadful sense of foreboding. The man behind the bench bore no resemblance to the short roly-poly judge they had expected.

She leaned toward Maitlin and clutched his arm. "What's going on? Who is this man, and where is the judge they assigned?"

Maitlin Culpin leaned back in his chair and steepled his fingers in front of him. "Seems as though they had a change of venue. It's not uncommon, but I have no grounds to object."

"But didn't you see her waving at him? My God, Jason probably had her sleep with this man to get my son away."

Bile rose in her throat and she considered running from the courtroom.

"Calm down, Callie. Not all judges can be bought so easily." He jotted something down on his tablet then turned his attention to the front of the courtroom.

Callie watched the judge rifle through a file folder of papers and click his teeth several times. Her heart raced and her mouth went dry. Several times the judge looked at her and nodded his head. "What is he doing?"

Maitlin shushed her.

"Ms. Carpenter, I've been reading over some files I received as reference to your character and I have to tell you I am a little concerned about the welfare of the child in question."

Callie stared at him, but her attorney spoke.

"Your Honor, I don't recall offering any such documents for the courts appraisal."

"They didn't come from your office, Mr. Culpin. And in my courtroom, you'll not speak until spoken to."

The judge turned his attention back to the papers in

question. After several more minutes, he lay the folder down in front of him. "Mr. Cuplin, you may make your opening remarks now, please."

Callie listened solemnly as her attorney made their arguments. He spoke of love, stability and loyalty. He reminded the judge of the importance of a mother to a child, and he pointed out that Cameron knew no other life.

When he finished the judge turned to Jason's attorney. The man spoke of money and material possessions. Not once during his speech did he mention anything about love. There was no comment made about whether or not her son would be happy in his new home. The cold fish of a man went on about how important it was that Jason have *his* son with him. Callie held the tears back as long as she could, before letting them slip down her cheeks and over her trembling lips.

"Well, I've heard enough. This court will recess for fifteen minutes while I reach my decision." He hammered the desk with his gavel and they all stood.

"Maitlin, why isn't he going to talk to Cameron?"

"I don't know. Maybe he doesn't need to. Let's just wait and see what he decides."

"I'm going to lose him. I can feel it."

A commotion in the back of the courtroom drew everyone's attention. Callie's heart pounded in her chest when Maitlin's secretary led Patric into the courtroom. They sat in the very last row of seats. Hushed whispers echoed around the room as everyone speculated about what would bring out the city's most reclusive man.

The bailiff instructed the room to rise as the judge made his way back into the courtroom. He situated himself in his chair and stared out over the courtroom. "I've reached a decision. It was not made in haste and I feel it is in the best interest of the boy."

Maitlin took Callie's hand in his and they listened as the judge droned on. Finally he said it.

"I find in favor of Mr. Carpenter." The judge paused. "I am awarding full custody to the father."

Callie didn't even try to hold back the scream building up her throat. She jumped out of her seat and reached across the table. Her lungs burned as one agonizing wail followed another.

The tears in her eyes turned to acid as they burned down her cheeks. "No!"

"Callie, stop. He'll toss you out."

"You can't take my baby."

The beating of the gavel against wood echoed in her head as she continued to cry out.

"Get your client under control or I'll cite you all for contempt of court. I won't stand for such childish outbursts in my courtroom."

Pain seared through her insides and her muscles tightened in protest to her actions. Her nails dug at the marred wood table and her palms stung from slapping the surface. "He can't do this." She turned toward Maitlin and he caught her in his arms as she collapsed. "Patric?" She cried out his name again and again.

"Callie, I'm right here." She looked up to find him standing over her.

Maitlin pushed his chair back and Sandra led Patric between them. He turned his attention to the judge. "I'm sorry your Honor. My client is obviously distraught over such an unfair decision."

"Don't you dare question me in my own courtroom. Furthermore, I am changing my decision to award unlimited visitation for Ms. Carpenter, and ordering only supervised visits."

Callie sobbed out loud as the judge tore her life into shreds of nothingness. With each order issued she lost something more. Something inside her snapped and she pushed away from Patric and struggled to get to Jason. "You son of a bitch! You stole my son. You paid off the judge. Didn't you?"

"Callie, stop it. This isn't helping." Maitlin pleaded with her to calm down, but she couldn't find the will to stop herself.

"Look at him, he doesn't care that he got custody. He only cares that he's taken one more thing from me."

Patric pulled her against him and she settled against his chest. The beating of his heart drew her in. She breathed in the scent of him and struggled for control. She ignored the rest of what the judge had to say and concentrated on breathing. Beat after beat her grasp slipped away. When the judge finally finished his lecture on how she should reevaluate her lifestyle and try to establish some stability before bringing more children into the world, he stood and left the courtroom.

"Callie, we're going to appeal and we'll get Cameron back. What I need from you now, is strength. I need you in good shape to show the court system you're a good mother."

"I am," Callie sobbed. Her body shook and her eyes burned as tears continued to fall. "Why couldn't he see that?"

Patric pulled her against his chest and she sighed.

CHAPTER ELEVEN

After a silent ride home, Sandra helped Callie and Patric into the house. Callie let herself be lead through the house and into her room. Sandra helped her out of her suit and tucked her into bed. The afternoon slipped away as Callie waited for her life to end. Without Cameron, she had no reason to go on.

The sun rose and set, but she remained secluded in her room.

Every day for a week, Patric came in and sat with her. They never spoke. He never touched her. He simply sat in the chair next to her bed and stared in her direction. On the seventh night, she waited for him to leave before climbing out her bed and going to lock the door before moving to stand by the window.

Small drops of rain splattered onto the patio. The soft pattering sounds soothed her into a trance. She stared up at sky and watched the stars flash in the darkness. Each blinking light reminded her of Cameron's eyes. With the thoughts of her son, she sank down onto her knees next to the French door and wept.

She tried to remember the last night she hadn't cried. Her happy days existed an eternity away. Lost in her own misery, she tried to ignore the knocking on her door.

"Callie, can I come in? It's important."

"Go away. There's nothing you can do and nothing

matters."

"Callie, you have a phone call." She sighed and covered her ears with her hands. "Go away!"

His fist against the door shook it until she thought she would scream. She ran to the door and fumbled with the lock. "I said I don't want—"

"Honey, Cam is on the phone."

Patric held the cordless phone in front of him.

Callie stared at it for several long moments before wiping her cheeks and grabbing it away from him. "Cameron, honey. Is it really you?" His tiny voice jarred her.

"Mom, you have to come and get me. He's going crazy."

Fear drove all reason from her and she clutched the phone. "Tell me what's wrong, honey." She could barely hear the soft words as he cried them into the telephone. Jason had come home drunk and picked a fight with Isabelle. When she refused to do what he wanted he'd hit her. Cameron rushed out his pleas as he explained Jason's drunken tirade in scant detail.

"Mom, I'm scared he is gonna hurt us. I like Belle, and I don't want him to hurt her."

Patric's words interrupted her and she remembered he still stood in the hallway. "What's wrong?"

"We need to go get Cameron."

Patric sighed and Callie turned to glare at him. The calm expression on his face pushed all the wrong buttons. "Don't you dare look at me like I'm crazy."

"Callie—"

The hurt in his voice anchored her. He couldn't look at her with pity or frustration. He couldn't see her. "I'm sorry."

He had no idea that her cheeks might be flushed from the fear and anger roiling around inside her. The truth of the matter, he couldn't do a damn thing to help her. She'd have to get her son on her own.

"Callie, what is it you want to do?" Patric stepped into the room and reached for the chair to his left.

"Jason is drunk and Cameron says he's become violent. I have to go get my baby." Callie put the phone back to her mouth and spoke to her son. "I'm going to come and get you right now. Where is he at the minute?"

"He's in the kitchen yelling at Belle. I'm scared for her, Mommy."

Callie rushed around the room gathering up her clothes. She slipped her feet into her pant legs and tugged them up. She scurried into her walk-in closet and came back out wearing a pair of slip-on loafers. Patric stood calmly behind the chair. "Cam, I'm going to hang up now. I am going to call the police and have them meet me there."

"Mom, he's gonna be mad if the police come."

"He'll get over it. I want you to go into your room and stay there until I come to get you. Do you promise?"

"I have to check on Belle."

"No, Cameron," she cried frantically. "Go to your room. Isabelle will be okay, I promise."

She hung up the phone and dialed 911. After explaining her situation to the dispatcher she tossed the phone on the bed and headed out of her room.

"Callie?"

She stopped in the hallway. "I'm going, and you can't stop me."

"Aren't you forgetting something?" Patric didn't

move.

"No, and I don't have time to play games with you."

"I'm going with you."

She hadn't expected that. "You can't."

Patric turned and walked toward her. "Then I'll find my own way there."

"Patric, I can't be worrying about both of you." She darted toward the stairs without giving him a chance to respond.

He was at the top of the stairs before she reached the landing. "Damn you, I love him too."

His revelation stopped her. As much as she'd longed to hear him say the words, she didn't have time to dwell on them. "I know." She rushed back up the stairs and took his hand in hers. "Well, hurry, I don't want the police to get there first. Cameron will be scared."

They rode to her ex husband's house in complete silence. When she pulled the car into the driveway her heart raced. Several police cars lined the drive. She jerked the car into park and jumped out. Several officers lined the porch, but the front door remained closed. She scooted past several other men who tried to hold her back. Pushing and clawing at the hands holding onto her, she fought with every ounce of her strength to get past them. As she reached the base of the porch a loud crash sounded. She heard Isabelle scream. With renewed determination, she reached for the doorknob.

"Callie, don't go in there. Let the police take care of it." Patric sounded calm, the total opposite of her own emotions.

Strong arms held her in place. "I have to get my son out of there. He's just a baby," Callie whispered hoarsely.

Another loud crash echoed out into the night and Callie turned into Patric's chest. "I can't stand this."

An officer stood off to the side of the front door and yelled in to Jason. Something slammed against the front door and everyone outside cringed and backed away. Cool drops of rain slipped down Callie's cheeks and she shivered. Patric held her tighter.

Finally, after several long minutes of coaxing, Jason jerked open the front door. He stood in the doorway with his terrified wife clutched against his chest. Callie's mind raced with all the memories of each time she'd been the one in his arms. Never had there been tenderness. Only anger and abuse. All of the nights Jason had used her only as a punching bag, bruising her flesh and inflicting the cruelest of emotional tortures on her. Her heart cried out for Isabelle.

"Jason, let her go. She's so young, and she can't fight you."

"What the hell are you doing here, Callie? You can't see my son unless I say you can." His words rolled together and she barely understood him. "You're not coming anywhere near him. Ever."

"Jason, why are you so mad? Did I do something to upset you?" Callie knew his drill. He'd probably done something he couldn't undo and needed someone else to shoulder the blame for his mistake.

"Callie, what are you doing?" Patric tried to hold her, but she slipped out of his grasp.

She stepped toward Jason hesitantly. "I'm sorry. I know I'm a disappointment to you, but I can make it up to you."

She stared past Jason and Isabelle and watched Cameron make his way toward the kitchen. If he made it, he could slip out the back door and would be safe. If only Jason would take her bait.

"You never do anything right, Callie."

"I know, Jason." She stepped up onto the porch and Jason came toward her. He was wrong; she'd given birth to Cameron and nothing could be more right. Callie gasped when Isabelle's face came into the light. Dark purple bruises marred her ivory complexion, and her eyes had both swelled nearly shut. She tried to raise her hand, but Jason tugged it back down and she cried out.

"I can't believe my luck. Two stupid wives in one lifetime. My mother told me not to marry anyone out of my league, but I had to have you. Callie, I could have given you the world, but you wanted to be a stupid nurse."

"I'm sorry. I should have stayed home and taken care of you and the house. I could do that now."

Patric edged toward the porch and Callie struggled to keep Jason's attention.

"You don't want to do that. You're just mad because I have everything you want. Money, status, and the kid."

Several officers moved in closer, but Jason ignored them.

Callie lowered her voice. "You know what would make you feel better? I could give you one of those neck rubs you like so much."

His grasp on Isabelle loosened and Callie feared she might fall.

"It's about the only thing you can do right."

Callie held her hand out to him. "Then let me do that for you." She took a step closer and he tightened his grip on his hostage.

"You're up to no good. You always are. That's why you'll never be anything. You don't know how to play the game. You think I am so stupid as to let you get close to me?"

He grabbed Isabelle by the hair and spun her around to face him.

"Let the lady go, pal. This isn't doing anyone any good." One of the police officers raised his gun and pointed it directly at Jason.

"Jason, don't do this. We can work this out," Callie pleaded.

"You're as bad as she is. Did you think I wouldn't find out about all the time you spent with those people behind my back?"

Isabelle hung in Jason's arms like a broken rag doll.

"I'm sorry, I didn't think a little bit of money would hurt."

"Why the hell should I pay for lazy people to live on the streets when it's none of my business?"

Callie didn't know what had set off Jason's tirade, but she needed to get him to let go of Isabelle before he really hurt her.

"You should have been more worried about taking care of the brat than all those people who don't know how to do a damn thing but sponge off people like me."

"Jason, I have been taking care of Cameron."

"Don't you talk back to me." He held her away from him and slapped her across the face. Several men moved in, but stopped their advance when he turned on them.

Cameron rushed the porch and flung himself at his father. "Don't you hit Belle. She hasn't done anything to you."

Callie turned her head in time to see Jason's hand make contact with the side of Cameron's face. The boy flew backward and landed on the wooden porch at Patric's feet. The effort it took to hit her son threw Jason off balance and Isabelle tumbled to the floor. Callie ignored her sobs and tried to get to Cameron, who also lay sobbing.

"Not so fast, you bitch." Jason grabbed her by the hair and Callie cried out.

Before anyone could react Jason pulled a gun from under his shirt and waved it wildly.

"Let go. You're hurting me, Jason." His other hand wrapped around her hair and he jerked her backward. The world began to spin and the pain threatened to overcome her.

Somewhere outside the haze of her pain the situation worsened, and chaos erupted on the porch. Familiar voices echoed in her head as she struggled to stay even a little bit coherent.

"Jason, let her go!" Patric shouted.

He didn't know what he could do, but he couldn't stand by and let this maniac beat the hell out of everyone around him. "You're a sick son of a--"

"Oh, you've got to be kidding me. You sorry excuse for a man. What do you think you can do to make me?"

Jason flung Callie away and advanced on Patric.

The sound of his footsteps on the wood planks told more than any of them could have guessed. Finally, Patric smelled the rancid odor of the man's breath in his face. Since the breath came straight at him, he guessed Jason was directly in front of him. He pulled back his arm and with lightning speed and a moment of prayer, he rammed it into the drunk man's ribs. He hadn't guessed Jason to be so short. He assumed from his attitude he would be considerably taller.

He stood still expecting to receive a return punch,

when it didn't come he stepped back. A flurry of activity erupted around him, but he remained still. Several times rough hands pushed him out of the way. For a moment he wondered if anyone remembered he existed.

"Patric?" Callie's voice sounded hoarse and dry. "Get Cameron."

A moment later Cameron flung himself into his arms. Patric held him against his chest and hugged him tight. "You're all right, son."

"He's not your son. He's my son, and you won't ever have him."

Jason's voice grew distant as Patric listened to him being hauled off by the police. He listened as the wheels of a stretcher clicked against the porch floor. Callie moaned and his heart throbbed.

"No, I'm all right. Please take care of Isabelle. She's been unconscious for so long."

For nearly an eternity Callie and Cameron had answered a multitude of questions. Detectives and paramedics talked and examined them both. She watched silently as they dressed Patric's scraped knuckles. She hardly believed that the only man who had been able to take down Jason was blind. Finally, the ambulance pulled off and headed to the hospital with Isabelle in it.

Callie sat in the front seat of the car and held Cameron. He'd made her go to the hospital to check on Isabelle before he would agree to go home. The entire way across town he'd sobbed and cried and questioned why his father had been so angry.

"Honey, he just isn't very good at sharing, and when Belle wanted to take care of all those people, he felt left out."

Cameron looked up at her. "It's my fault, mom." He lowered his head.

"No, honey, that's not true. Your father has some problems and they have nothing to do with you."

"You don't understand. I made Belle do it. I wanted to go away, and I saw on television that you could do nice things for people, so I begged her to take me to the big house and help those people."

Callie's heart sang out. Her son had volunteered to help homeless people, even if his motives weren't totally pure, he'd made the effort. "I think it is wonderful that you and Isabelle did this."

"Belle is really nice, and I hope she'll be okay. He hurt her like he hurt you, mom." He reached up and rubbed his fingers along her bruised jaw line. She held herself from jerking away from his clumsy touch. The gesture of concern touched her too deeply to betray it. "Does it hurt much?"

"No, hardly at all. I'm a mom, I can take it." Callie looked up to find Patric and her attorney, Maitlin, standing next to the car. "So, what do we do now?"

"Well, sorry as I am that this happened, it's been your miracle. I found a new judge to sign an order granting you immediate and permanent custody of Cameron."

"Oh thank heaven." Callie pulled Cameron against her and sobbed openly. She let him go only when Patric touched her shoulder.

"I owe you so much."

Patric blushed and she enjoyed the pleased look on his face. She'd missed his sharp wit and his handsome scowl. The crease in his forehead she'd thought to be permanent, had almost disappeared in a matter of hours. For the first time since she'd met him, his face looked peaceful.

"You don't owe me anything. I promised you I would help you and I did as much as I could."

"Patric, you knocked Jason flat on his—"

"Rear," Cameron finished. "It was really cool how you punched him. How did you know where to hit him?"

"I don't know, Cam. All I did know is that I had to do something to help you and your mom, and that is what happened."

"Do you love me and my mom?" Cameron waited for the answer.

"Cameron Carpenter, don't be so rude."

"It's okay, I think it's a fair question. As a matter of fact, I do."

Cameron tugged on his mother's sleeve. "See, I knew he loved us."

Callie's eyes grew wide and her breath caught in her throat. Every time she opened her mouth to speak, sensible thought flew out before she could manage it. It couldn't possibly be true. He'd made no effort to keep her from leaving and he'd made no effort to get her back. They'd spent an entire week cooped up in his house and he hadn't so much as spoken to her until tonight. He couldn't possibly love her.

"Callie when you walked out of my hospital room I thought my life had ended. I couldn't imagine my life without you."

"But—"

"But I am too much of a fool to know I should have fought for you sooner," he interrupted. "I let myself believe you could never love me." His mouth opened and then closed. His face turned a pasty shade of white. "God, I'm so stupid. I never even bothered to ask if you loved me."

Callie laughed. She laughed so hard Cameron nearly fell out of her lap. Her eyes teared up and she swiped at them with the back of her hand.

"Of course she loves you, silly." Cameron pushed his shoulder playfully and Patric laughed.

"Mom, why are you crying?" Cameron held her face in his hands. "Mom?"

"He is silly." She laughed. "He is the silliest man I have ever met in my whole entire life."

"I beg your pardon." Patric stood motionless.

"Of course I love you," she whispered. "I think I've loved you all along. Why else would I put up with your horrible attitude and your need to fire me on a weekly basis?"

"Have I been that bad?"

"Yep!" Callie and Cameron answered at the same time.

"I guess I just didn't realize I couldn't live without— the two of you." He held out his hand and Cameron took it in his.

"Patric, do you think we could get married?" Cameron looked up at the man before him with open admiration. He'd never had that bond with Jason.

"Well, kiddo, I think maybe your mom and I should work that out. But I promise you will be the first to know what we decide."

Cameron flew out of her lap and into his arms. The pair looked natural together and Callie's heart raced with joy.

"Let's go home."

Patric waited for Callie to come and help him into the car. The ride home took an eternity to Patric, but he would wait however long it took to show Callie how much he loved her.

It took hours for Callie to calm her son enough for him to fall asleep. Patric paced along the study carpet and waited for his turn with her. Finally, the study door opened and he heard her enter the room. He inhaled the scent of her rose water perfume and listened to the unfamiliar rustle of fabric. He couldn't quite place it.

"I'm sorry it took so long. I wanted to make sure he was completely asleep before I left him alone."

He listened in amazement at the calmness in her voice. Six hours earlier she'd been on the brink of hysteria. So much had happened in such a short time. For all of them. "It's okay. I put the time to good use."

"And how did you do that?"

She stepped up close to him and he realized what fabric he'd been hearing.

"What are you wearing?"

Callie leaned against him and whispered into his ear. "See for yourself."

"Callie, you know perfectly well that—"

She giggled against his neck and he sighed out loud. She took his hand in hers and placed it on her hip. His body took control and he did what came naturally.

First, his hand slid down over her hip and caressed her upper thigh. Then he slowly moved it back up the length of her side until his thumb brushed against her hard nipple. The sound of her breathing tripped his nerves and his knees went weak. In his whole life he'd never been so unsure of what to do, but her hands on his shoulders eased that insecurity. One second rolled into the next as his hands slid gently along the satin fabric of her very short nighty. More than once he thought his legs would give out.

"I love you too." Her words wrapped around him like a cocoon of safety. He buried his face in her hair and breathed in the love emanating from her very body. She wrapped her arms around his waist and they stood alone in their own world until he couldn't stand it anymore. He had so much to tell her and he needed to do it before they went any further.

"Callie, I've made some decisions and I need to tell you about them." He held her away from him, but kept her hands in his. "I'm not sure in what order to do this, so I'll just say it."

She didn't speak, but lead him to the sofa by the window.

"I want to marry you."

"Oh, Patric, I want that too."

"But I can't." He heard her breath catch. "Wait, there's more."

Callie sighed. "I certainly hope so."

I can't marry you until I do something."

Patric spent the next hour convincing Callie that he had made up his mind and he hoped with all his heart she would stand by him. He finally breathed again when she hugged him tightly.

EPILOGUE

Patric woke to a horrible throbbing in his head. He remembered being awake several times over the last few days, but each time he'd let the pain take him back to sleep.

This time he forced himself to stay awake. A flood of memories came rushing back. A man standing over him, his breath muffled by a surgical mask. Then quiet. He imagined some might have remembered the darkness, but his life consisted of darkness. A door opened and he turned toward the creaking. "Hello?"

"Good afternoon, Mr. LeClerc. I'm Doctor Paulson. I think it's time we see how good I am at my job."

Patric's heart stopped and he knew the moment of truth had finally arrived. He'd discussed the transplant with Callie in great detail. They'd agreed to go ahead and no matter what the outcome, Callie would be waiting for him at the altar on Valentine's day.

"What's the date?" Patric asked.

"February thirteenth. I know about your date, and if everything has gone according to schedule I'll authorize you to go to the hospital chapel."

"Has she been here?" Patric didn't remember anyone coming or going from his room for several days, but then again, the pain had left him senseless.

"She finally left this morning when we threatened to admit her into her own room. Now, what do you say we get rid of some of these bandages?"

Patric eased himself into a sitting position and waited for the next move. Cold hands brushed against his cheeks as the eye surgeon unwrapped layers of bandages. With each second that passed he grew more frightened. What if he still couldn't see? Would Callie really stay by his side?

"I want you to understand. Mr. LeClerc. You aren't going to be seeing twenty twenty, but you should be able to distinguish shapes and color tones. The nurses have been changing the bandages daily. "I don't want you to open your eyes until I say so."

"I'm ready." The cool air hit his eyes as the doctor removed the last bandage. It took all his control to keep his eyes closed, but he did as instructed.

"Slowly, I want you to open your eyes."

Patric held his breath. What would be worse, having partial vision restored, or still being blind? How could he face life knowing he'd lived through another failure? Self-doubt enveloped him and squeezed the air out of his lungs. He forced the doubts aside and opened his eyes. Greeted with darkness his spirits plunged downward in a spiral of defeat. He started to close them again.

"Keep them open. It might take a minute or two for you to focus."

Patric prayed. *God, give me this and—*

"Patric, can I come in?" Callie questioned from the doorway.

He turned his head and pain shot through his temple. But a moment later something incredible happened. He squeezed his eyes shut. "No, not yet. Wait out in the hall and I'll let you know when." The door closed again and he knew she'd left.

He leaned his head back and opened his eyes. The light from the window crept past his shadowed visions. He stared at the floral painting on the wall. It didn't appear clear, but the blur of the colors held him in awe. It had been too many years since he'd been annoyed by the splashy pinks of Monet wannabe paintings.

"I can see." Tears welled up in his eyes.

"Go ahead and cry, it'll help the healing process," the doctor instructed.

Patric sat patiently as the doctor and another nurse did a series of tests and took a tablet full of notes. When they finally left it was with instructions to have Callie make the last minute arrangements and to meet him in the chapel at sunset the next evening.

The music started and Patric walked out into the chapel. His only friends, Maitlin and Sandra stood beside him at the small altar. Patric gazed around the room, taking in every sight the cross, to the gleaming wooden railing. He gazed with wonder and amazement at the small boy beside him, holding what he could only guess to be Mardi the kitten.

Every few seconds Cameron would hold up his fingers. "How many this time?"

Patric smiled and patted his small round head. The boy's green eyes sparkled with pure excitement and his smile spoke his feelings louder than any words could.

The few people in the chapel turned their attention to the back of the room and his gaze followed theirs. Callie stood in the doorway. He squinted to get a clearer vision of her and his breath caught.

Long curls of auburn hair draped down around the perfectly shaped face. She took several steps toward him and her beauty glowed throughout the room. When she stopped next to him, she stared at him with emerald green eyes, eyes he thought surely did an emerald justice.

Tears glistened on her lashes when he reached up to stroke her cheek. He rubbed his thumb along her long lashes and down the narrow slope of her nose, a nose he'd only kissed once, but would spend a lifetime cherishing. He stared at her lips, lips he'd tasted with all the hunger of a man starving. He'd wanted to see her lips, her face, all of her. Now he could and he would never take his eyes off her again.

The ceremony passed in a flurry of garbled words and murmured responses from both of them. When the minister finally pronounced them man and wife, Patric could only gaze at the reflection of himself in her crystal clear eyes. He was handsome, not a scarred ruin of a man as he had imagined. And all the love he could ever have hoped for shone in her eyes. As he gazed into those emerald pools, before him lay the most incredible vision of his entire existence, his reason for living.

The warmth her smile bathed him in stirred him beyond measure. When he finally tasted the sweetness of his bride's mouth, he closed his eyes, and for the first time in years, he felt no fear of the dark. The brightness of their love blazed in his heart, through the darkness to bring him back into the light.

Welcome to the world of Domhan Books! Domhan, pronounced DOW-ann, is the Irish word for universe. Our vision is to provide readers with high-quality hardcover, paperback and electronic books in a variety of genres from writers all over the world.

ORDERING INFORMATION
All Domhan paper books may be ordered from Barnes and Noble, barnesandnoble.com, Amazon, Borders, and other fine booksellers using the ISBN. They are distributed worldwide by Ingram Book Group, 1 Ingram Blvd., La Vergne, Tennessee 37086 (615) 793-5000. Most titles are also available electronically in a variety of formats through Galaxy Library at www.galaxylibrary.com. Rocket *e*Book™ editions are available on-line at barnesand noble.com, Powell's, and other booksellers. Please visit our website for previews, reviews, and further details on our titles: www.domhanbooks.com. Domhan Books, 9511 Shore Road, Suite 514, Brooklyn, New York 11209 U.S.A.

ACTION AND ADVENTURE

Paladin - Barry Nugent 1-58345-365-2 192 pp. $12.95
Princess Yasmin must go on a quest for a mythical crown, the only thing that can prevent civil war erupting in the exotic land of Primera. Along the way she meets her favorite adventure author Barnaby Jackson, and the sparks really start to fly. This is a taut action novel reminiscent of the Indiana Jones series of films.

Yala - Don Clark 1-58345-561-2 180 pp. $12.95
In the no man's land between the U.S. and Mexico in

1896, a Chinese clan stakes a claim to a new territory. Two Texas Rangers decide to end their law officer careers and go to New China in order to raise the bankroll needed to start a ranch. Hank and his younger sidekick, Luke, soon meet Yala, a condemned and notorious Chinese criminal: a female assassin.

CHRISTIAN FICTION
The Way Found - Nina J. Lechiara 1-58345-017-3 472 pp. $20.00
1532-1558
Matteo and Gianna search for love and truth in university studies, religion and philosophy, from Padua and Venice to Egypt and Arabia. They find it unexpectedly in Yahshua, in the one place they have never looked, the Scriptures. They learn both the truth and the meaning of love and marriage, and become shining examples of Yahvah's way.

FANTASY
The Druid's Woman - Shanna Murchison 1-58345-245-1 120 pp. $10
In this novel of Ireland, Davnat encounters Parthalann, a mysterious druid who trains her up to be his helper and consort. But despite all the powers she is given, their Fates have already been decreed....

The Wizard Woman - Shanna Murchison 1-58345-020-3 204 pp. hardcover $18.95; 1-58345-018-1 paper $12.95
Ireland 1169
The great Celtic myth of the Wheel of Fate is played out against the backdrop of the first Norman invasion of Ireland in 1169. Dairinn is made the wizard's woman, chosen by the gods to be the wife of the handsome but mysterious Senan. Through him she discovers her own innate powers, and the truth behind her family history. She must bargain with the Morrigan, the goddess of death, if she is ever to

achieve happiness with the man she loves. But how high a price will she have to pay for Senan's life?

The Wings of Love - Karen L. Williams   1-58345-466-7   180 pp. $12.95
There is no room in Sean MacDonagh's life for imagination. But when he finds himself having the same dreams over and again, he has to do something, and quickly. The last thing he considers as good therapy is a trip to Northern Ireland to see his estranged family. Then again, getting away from the hustle and bustle of New York City might be just what he needs to clear his mind of the mysterious woman who begins to haunt his whole life.
Treyanna, Faerie princess, rebelling against an arranged marriage, travels through time to win her freedom. Completely opposite to Sean in every way, the time they spend together brings them all they are missing in their lives. But can Sean learn to live with Treyanna's mystical powers, or will he flee from her-and his own insecurities and failings?

HISTORICAL FICTION
The Wildest Heart - Jacinta Carey   1-58345-041-6   224 pp. $12.95
Rebecca Whitaker is struggling to keep her family ranch from foreclosure by trading with the Indians, working in a saloon, and breeding horses. Enter the mysterious Walker Pritchard, claiming he wishes to stay with Reb to leave the memories of the Civil War behind and learn about the ways of the west. They fall in love, but can Reb trust Walker? What are his real motives for coming to the Bar T, and how did he know there would be gold in those hills? Reb must fight to save him and her ranch, before everything she loves is destroyed by the men from Walker's mysterious past.

Natchez - Deb Crockett   1-58345-008-4   180 pp. $12.95

Welcome to Natchez, home to whores, gamblers, and anyone out to make a fast buck, no matter what the cost...
The untimely death of lovely young Rebecca Bennett's father forces the feisty girl from Savannah to live by her wits. Alone, penniless, and seemingly betrayed by the only man she has ever truly loved, she struggles to stay alive and fulfill her dream: to buy her beloved Oliver's plantation and have a home of her own, even though he is miles away. But though she tries to live honestly through hard work, she makes powerful enemies. Can she ever find happiness, safety, love, and the people responsible for her father's death and her ruin?

The Summer Stars - Alan Fisk   1-58345-549-3   202 pp. $12.95
Britain's oldest poems were composed in the sixth century by the bard Taliesin. Many legends have been told about he of the "shining brow," but in this novel he tells his own story. Taliesin's travels take him through turbulent times as Britain tries to cope with the disappearance of Roman civilization, and the increasing threat of the Saxon invaders.

Scars Upon Her Heart - Sorcha MacMurrough   1-58345-011-4   232 pp. $12.95
Lady Vevina Joyce and her brother Wilfred are forced to flee Ireland after being falsely accused of treason. On the road with Wellington's army, they meet an unexpected ally in the enigmatic Major Stewart Fitzgerald. Side by side they fight with their comrades in some of the most bitter battles of the Napoleonic Wars. Can Vevina clear her name, protect those she loves, and stop the Grand Army from taking over the whole of Europe in a bold and daring move engineered by the person responsible for her family's disgrace? Is Stewart really all that he seems? Appearances can be deceptive....

**Destiny Lies Waiting - Diana Rubino   1-58345-078-5 hardcover   208 pp. $18.50;
1-58345-451-9 paper $12.95
Volume One of** *The Yorkist Saga*
Beautiful orphaned Denys has been bought up a member of the Woodville family, now in power thanks to her aunt Elizabeth, wife of the new Yorkist king Edward IV. Unwilling to become a pawn in her aunt's bid for power, she decides to seek the truth about her family and identity.
Valentine Starbury, loyal ally to young Richard, Duke of Gloucester, the King's brother, agrees to woo Denys in order to save his friend from Elizabeth Woodville's plan for Richard and Denys to wed. He unexpectedly falls in love with her, thus earning the enmity of the queen. The secrets both uncover will have dangerous consequences for Denys and Valentine, and the whole of England itself.

**Thy Name is Love - Diana Rubino   1-58345-079-3 hardcover   212 pp. $18.50;
1-58345-392-X   paper $12.95
Volume Two of** *The Yorkist Saga*
The story first begun in *Destiny Lies Waiting* continues in this second volume. Denys Starbury and her husband Valentine are thrust into the world of power politics as one by one the royal family is eliminated, until only one man can contend for the throne, Richard, Duke of Gloucester. Denys continues to search for her lost family, but she finds only a trail of murder and destruction. She also seeks the love of Valentine. In a world of shifting allegiances, how can she ever bring herself to trust him?

**The Jewels of Warwick - Diana Rubino   1-58345-080-7 hardcover   236 pp. $18.50;   1-58345-413-6 paper $12.95
Volume Three of** *The Yorkist Saga*
In this sequel to *Thy Name is Love,* the saga of the Yorkist

royal family continues. The "Jewels" are two sisters, Topaz and Amethyst Plantagenet. They are descendants of Richard III, who lost his life and kingdom to Henry Tudor, future father of Henry VIII.

Topaz always felt she was the rightful queen, and would have been, had her father been crowned as Richard's heir. But life holds many strange twists of fate....

Crown of Destiny - Diana Rubino   1-58345-081-5 hardcover   204 pp. $18.50;
1-58345-456-X paper $12.95
Volume Four of *The Yorkist Saga*
In this sequel to *The Jewels of Warwick*, Topaz's rebellion against Henry VIII gets under way, throwing England into civil war and chaos. Amethyst is forced to choose between remaining loyal to her sister, or losing the only two men she has ever loved: the king, and her sister's husband Matthew....

I Love You Because - Diana Rubino   1-58345-082-3 hardcover   264 pp. $18.50;
1-58345-423-3 paper   264 pp. $12.95
Vita Caputo meets handsome Irish cop Tom McGlory at the scene of a crime. This fateful encounter has consequences for both their families as they must struggle together to end the corruption in turn-of-the-century New York City politics before more crimes are committed and more lives are lost.

An Experience in Four Movements - Lidmila Sovakova   1-58345-002-5   124 pp. $10
This is a historical puzzle situated in the seventeenth century. Its pieces reconstruct the infatuation of a Poet with a Princess, culminating in the death of the Poet, and the retreat of the Princess within the walls of a monastery.

IRISH INTEREST
Call Home the Heart - Sorcha MacMurrough 1-58345-072-6 hardcover 244 pp. $18.95; 1-58345-394-6 paper $12.95
Young widow Muireann Graham Caldwell is left destitute by her dissolute husband, Augustine, killed in a shooting accident on their honeymoon. Faced with a choice between returning to her stifling parents in Scotland or taking a chance on running her own estate, Muireann finds an ally in the broodingly handsome Lochlainn Roche. He has secrets of his own to keep. As the Potato Famine rages across Ireland, can Muireann save her new home Barnakilla? Can she and her estate manager ever have a future together? Does he even love her? Or has he been using her all along?

The Faithful Heart - Sorcha MacMurrough 1-58345-023-8 204 pp. $12.95
Who has murdered Morgana Maguire's brother, poisoned her father, and stolen most of her clan's ships? These are just a few of the pressing questions Morgana must find answers to if she and her one true love Ruairc MacMahon are ever to find happiness in each other's arms. Set against the backdrop of Renaissance power politics during the reign of Henry VIII, Morgana and Ruairc must fight not only to win each other, but also to protect all of Ireland from civil war and foreign invasion.

The Fire's Centre - Sorcha MacMurrough 1-58345-025-4 264 pp. $12.95
Riona Connolly is willing to do anything to save her family from starvation during the Potato Famine. So when she meets the handsome Dr. Lucien Woulfe, who offers her post at his clinic, it seems a dream come true. But their growing attraction is forbidden in the straight-laced society of Victorian Dublin. Riona and Lucien must walk through the

fire's centre to secure their happiness before it is destroyed by the evil Dr. O'Carroll and the vagaries of Fate.

The Hart and the Harp - Sorcha MacMurrough   1-58345-030-0   288 pp. $12.95
Ireland, 1149
Shive MacDermot and Tiernan O'Hara agree to wed to end a five-year feud between their clans. Though an unlikely alliance at first, Shive begins to fall in love with her new husband. She soon realises the murderer of her brother is a member of her own clan. How can she win Tiernan's love and prove to him she is not the enemy? Shive undertakes an epic struggle to save her lands and Tiernan's from the ambitious Muireadach O'Rourke, determined to kill anyone who opposes his bid to become high-king of all Ireland. Will she prove worthy of Tiernan, or will he believe all of the vicious lies about her supposed love for another, and become her enemy himself?

Hunger for Love - Sorcha MacMurrough   1-58345-005-X   244 pp. $12.95
Ireland and Canada, 1847
Emer Nugent and her family are evicted from their home at the height of the Potato Famine in Ireland. Forced to emigrate to Canada, they endure a harrowing journey on board a coffin ship bound for Grosse Ile. Emer, working as a cabin boy to help her family's financial situation, meets the enigmatic Dalton Randolph, the ship's only gentleman passenger, who is not all that he seems. They fall in love, but darker forces are at work against them. Emer's duty to her family forces the lovers to separate. Will they ever be able to overcome the obstacles in their path to true love? This incredible saga of love, adventure and intrigue continues in the second volume *The Hungry Heart*.

The Hungry Heart - Sorcha MacMurrough   1-58345-006-8   232 pp. $12.95
Canada and Ireland 1847-1849
Emer Nugent leaves her lover Dalton Randall to search for her family in the hell of the Grosse Ile quarantine station. The land of opportunity is nearly the death of them all. Dalton is deceived by his father into thinking Emer is dead, and is about to marry the daughter of a business rival when he meets Emer again. Outraged that his plans for keeping the two apart have failed,
Dalton's father has Emer arrested on false charges and transported back to Ireland.
But the Ireland she returns to is on the brink of civil war. Emer finds herself unwittingly embroiled in the 1848 rebellion, and is put on trial for her life. Dalton must travel half way across the world to try to save her before it is too late. This incredible saga of love and adventure begins with the first volume, *Hunger for Love.*

The Sea of Love - Sorcha Mac Murrough 1-58345-032-7 6 hardcover 148 pp. $15.95; 1-58345-033-5 paper $10
Ireland 1546
Wrongfully accused of murder, Aidanna O'Flaherty's only ally against her evil brother-in-law Donal is the dashing English-bred aristocrat Declan Burke. Saving him from certain death, they fall in love, only to be separated when Declan is falsely accused of treason. Languishing in the Tower, Declan is powerless to assist his beloved Aidanna as she undertakes an epic struggle to expose her enemy and save her family and friends. She must race against time to prevent all she loves from being swept aside in a thunderous tide of foreign invasion....

<u>MYSTERY</u>
St. John's Baptism - William Babula 1-58345-496-9 260 pp. $12.95
In this first of the Jeremiah St. John series, the hero is sum-

moned to a meeting by Rick Silverman, one of San Francisco's most prominent drug attorneys. St. John knows Silverman's unsavory clientele and so does not think anything of the invitation—that is until he finds Silverman dead.

According to St. John - William Babula 1-58345-521-9 240 pp. $12.95
In this second St. John adventure, St. John's friend Denise is supposed to be in Frisco appearing in a new production of *Macbeth* with legendary actress Amanda Cole. They arrive at the theater only to discover that Amanda has been murdered and Denise is the prime suspect. St. John soon learns that everyone involved is playing a role. By the time they track down the killer, St. John and his intrepid colleagues uncover some horrifying secrets from the past, and the mind-boggling motive.

St. John and the Seven Veils - William Babula   1-58345-506-X 208 pp. $12.95
In this third mystery in the popular series, St John and his two partners Mickey and Chief Moses are hired to track down a serial killer by a woman claiming to be the killer's mother! Three men have been brutally murdered, but they are without any apparent connection until St. John stumbles across one through a seemingly unrelated case. From the Seven Veils Brothel in Reno to a hideout in Northern California, St John is hot on the trail, crossing paths with a famous televangelist, prominent military man, high-powered doctor, and a complete madman.

St. John's Bestiary - William Babula - 1-58345-511-6 264 pp. $12.95
St. John should never have taken this fourth case. But he just couldn't help it—Professor Krift's story of his eight stolen cats strikes a sympathetic chord. After rescuing the vic-

tims from a ruthless gang of animal rights activists, the CFAF, he is caught catnapping as the CFAF kidnap the professor's daughter. Suddenly the morgue is filling up, and not just with strangers. St. John's new love Ollie is killed, and he determines to stop at nothing until her murder is avenged. The tangled case drags him through every racket going: money laundering, dope pushing, porno, prostitution, and very nearly drags him six foot under.

St. John's Bread - William Babula 1-58345-516-7 hardcover 180 pp. $18.95;
1-58345-516-7 paper $12.95
In this fifth volume of the series, St. John and his two intrepid partners get caught up in a tangle of missing children's cases after he and Mickey rescue a baby about to be kidnapped in a public park. Mickey tries to tell him that he needs the "bread" to pay for his brand new Victorian stately home which houses him and their detective agency, but this case comes with a higher price tag than any of them are willing to pay.

The Fox and the Puma - Barbara Sohmers 1-58345-486-1 156 pp. $10
This is the first novel in the popular Fred and Maggy Renard series.
When a nude, partly-devoured body is found near a popular beach on an island off the southern coast of France, the small community erupts into panic. Old hatreds and sins begin to surface, and many more ugly secrets will be revealed...

The Fox and the Pussycat - Barbara Sohmers 1-58345-491-8 160 pp. $10
In the second of her Fred and Maggy Renard adventures, the intrepid pair become embroiled in the raunchy underground world of Paris in an effort to track down the killer of her friend Marie-Claude.

ROMANCES
Campaign for Love - Michaela Brennan   1-58345-285-0   144 pp. $10
Tired of being hassled over her gorgeous looks, Suzanna Sills dresses down to get a wonderful new job in a top-notch ad agency. She soon regrets her frumpy appearance when she has to work with the gorgeous Quentin Pierce. Quentin hasn't failed to notice that his hottest new star has more to her than meets the eye. But office intrigues get them both into a spin. Can they avoid losing the biggest ad campaign the company has ever seen, and learn to trust one another?

The Right Code - Sharon Holmes   1-58345-448-9 $12.95
Jonathan C. Evans is mocked as a computer nerd who lives by logic. Jasmine Banks is the only one who sees Jon differently. She grows determined to make this man realize that logic has nothing to do with a relationship between a man and a woman. But she gets more than she bargains for as the real JC Evans is revealed...

The Picture of Bliss - Jacqui Jerome 1-58345-268-0   168 pp. $10
Just when Candice Edwards thinks she has escaped from her past, she is propelled into a nightmarish encounter with her ex-fiancé. Can she trust the secretive and mercurial designer Lochlainn Alexander, or is he part of the whole plot to ruin her career?

Heart's Desire - Sorcha MacMurrough   1-58345-031-9   160 pp. $10
Nurse Sinead Thomas rescues the hospital's handsome architect Austin Riordan from a life-threatening situation. She accepts his offer to be his private nurse over the Christmas holidays, but gets more than she bargained for as they grow ever closer. A young widow, she never wants to go through the torment of being in love again. But Austin is nothing if

not persistent. Can they fight the demons from her past, to secure their hearts' desire?

Star Attraction - Sorcha MacMurrough   1-58345-037-8
168 pp. $10
Zaira Darcy literally bumps into the man of her dreams in an elevator. Dashing Brad Clarke, Hollywood's hottest new director, working alongside her in New York, is everything she could want in a man, and more. But the secrets from her past, and the double life she leads, threaten to destroy any chance of happiness the two might have. Zaira must lock horns with her ex-husband Jonathan one last time to save Brad's life, even if it means sacrificing her own.

The Marriage Contract - Lisa Mondello 1-58345-471-3
148 pp. $12.95
Cara Carvalho and Devin Michaels became best friends one distant summer, until fate and their own inner needs for success forced them to separate. Now both are seeking more from their lives. A glib promise on the back of her seventeenth birthday card is enough to bring them together again. Can they have a second chance at happiness?

Nothing But Trouble - Lisa Mondello 1-58345-349-0 120 pp. $10
Melanie Summers, a feisty zoologist with big dreams, must spend a month in the Wyoming wilderness in order to satisfy a deal made with her father. Stoney Buxton is a hard-driving cowboy with simple values who needs to raise money to save the family ranch. To everyone else, her offer seems like the answer to all his prayers. But one look at her long legs and pouting lips and Stoney know this high society gal is going to be nothing but trouble for his cowboy heart.

Love's Sweet Song - Annabelle Stevens   1-58345-275-3
132 pp. $10

Angelica Castle Murray loses everything in a tragic accident: husband, daughter, and very nearly her life. But in the aftermath of his disaster, she must not only struggle to regain her health, but to come to terms with the fact that ever since her ex-fiancé Winston broke up with her seven years before, she has been living a lie. Winston Murray has never stopped loving Angelica, even when she was married to his brother. Her old life is now in shambles; but how can he tell her that her life with Oliver has been a big lie?

The Art of Love - Evelyn Trimborn 1-58345-001-7 164 pp. $10
Struggling Dublin artist Shannon Butler gives a hugely successful show. Enter her estranged adopted brother Marius Winters, hell-bent on revenge. He accuses her of robbing him of his share of their dead father's estate. Thrown together by circumstances, they try to make up for the mistakes of the past. Despite all their differences, they grow ever closer. But Marius' lying ex-wife threatens any chance of happiness they might have. How can Shannon prevent her new-found love from leaving her forever?

Castles in the Air - Evelyn Trimborn 1-58345-019-X 168 pp. $10
Poverty-stricken aristocrat Alanna Lacy is at her wits' end. Enter property developer Bran Ryan, who offers her a way out of her desperate financial situation—marry him! Faced with her father's disapproval, and Bran's spiteful ex-fiancée, can they build a future together, or will all their dreams go up in smoke?

Forbidden Fantasy - Evelyn Trimborn 1-58345-256-7 124 pp. $10
Rose Gray is one of America's top romance writers. So why is it she can't ever seem to meet Mr. Right? Luke Byrnes

changes all that when he bursts into her life unexpectedly. Will it be "Happily Ever After" Or "The End"?

Heedless Hearts - Evelyn Trimborn   1-58345-251-6   132 pp. $10
Inexperienced housekeeper Marielle gets more than she bargains for when she takes a post at the house of architect Tristan Fitzmaurice. Sparks fly from the moment they meet, but all too soon, she can feel herself being drawn to him irresistibly. But how can she love him, when he is about to be married to another? But the heart is heedless when it comes to love.

Design for Love - Shirley Wolford   1-58345-594-9 $10
Beautiful interior decorator Ann Seymour gets the chance to prove herself more than capable of running her family's design works when she runs into the enigmatic Adam Frazier, a swashbuckling hunk who has lived abroad for many years and returned home to Orange County. She has a job to do, but can she ever learn to control her feelings whenever they meet?

THRILLERS
The Delaney Escape - Brent Kroetch   1-58345-021-1   264 pp. $12.95
Ex-CIA agent turned IRA man Noel Delaney plans to escape from Leavenworth prison.
Guy Morgan, an ex-agent trained by Delaney, is determined to track his old mentor down. He teams up with his longtime love, Karly Widman of British Intelligence, to trace Delaney's movements to Ireland. But the trap springs. Who is the hunter, and who the prey?

Ghost From the Past - Sorcha MacMurrough   1-58345-029-7   180 pp. $12.95

Biochemist Clarissa Vincent's fiancé Julian Simmons was killed in a terrible explosion five years ago. Or was he? Taking a new job in Portland, Oregon, Clarissa sees a man at the airport who could be Julian's double, and is suddenly propelled into a nightmarish world of espionage and intrigue. She must struggle to save her family and the man she has always loved from the ruthless people who will stop at nothing to achieve world domination.

In From the Cold - Carolyn Stone   1-58345-007-6   224 pp. $12.95
Cambridge scientist Sophie Ruskin is dragged into a world of espionage and intrigue when her father, a Russian defector, vanishes. Adrian Vaughan, handsome, enigmatic, but haunted by his past, is assigned to train her as a spy to win her father's freedom, or destroy his work before his kidnappers can create the ultimate weapon. But Adrian's fate soon lies in Sophie's hands, as she travels two continents to save his life, win his love, and fight for the freedom of the oppressed, war-torn Russian Republic of Chechnya.

Mutual Attraction - Diana Waldhuber 1-58345-382-2 148 pp. $10
Journalist Jordan Taylor's dream job turns out to be a nightmare when she meets the cool, suave, Ashford Blackard. Each presents an irresistible challenge for the other—but what will the fateful consequences of their game of cat and mouse be?

Spin Me a Web - Shirley K. Wolford   1-58345-598-1 $12.95
Caitlin Cameron, amateur sleuth and feature writer for *Antique Autos Magazine*, challenges her readers to find the thief who stole four priceless antique sports cars. Her life is threatened unless she stops her column. But she's stubborn and has other ideas. She asks Rick Falconer, world-class

tennis ace, and new owner of the romantic pre-war, hand-made, antique sports car, *the Princess Eula*, to help trap the thief by using his car as bait.

Rick is appalled at her request and refuses. But then the car is stolen and Rick becomes the main suspect. Both must work together to find the real thief, and uncover a conspiracy which threatens their blossoming love for one another.

WESTERNS
Rainbow's End - Shirley Wolford 1-58345-466-7 $12.95
Beautiful widow Prue Jamison saw a rainbow that stretched all the way from Boston to the newly discovered gold fields in California. Prue needed a new place to live, and there was nothing newer than San Francisco.

Ex-Captain Beau Graham wanted no part of a woman who ventured around Cape Horn without an escort. When the Mexican War ended, he had shed all his responsibilities and had no intention of taking on a beautiful, bold-spirited woman who was probably no better than she should be.

YOUNG ADULT FICTION
God's Children - Clarence Guenter Ages 10-12 years 1-58345-027-0 108 pp. $8
This is the heart-warming semi-autobiographical story of growing up in a Mennonite community in Canada in the late 1940s.

Shipwreck by Kristina Vance Ages: 12-16 years 1-58345-038-6 160 pp. $8
A mysterious craft crash-lands in a field near a lone homestead, propelling the family into an adventure beyond their wildest dreams....